The Meadowlark Sings

The Meadowlark Sings

Helen Ruth Schwartz

Alice Street Editions™
Harrington Park Press®
An Imprint of The Haworth Press, Inc.
New York • London • Oxford

For more information on this book or to order, visit
http://www.haworthpress.com/store/product.asp?sku=5559

or call 1-800-HAWORTH (800-429-6784) in the United States and Canada
or (607) 722-5857 outside the United States and Canada

or contact orders@HaworthPress.com

Published by

Alice Street Editions™, Harrington Park Press®, an imprint of The Haworth Press, Inc., 10
Alice Street, Binghamton, NY 13904-1580.

PUBLISHER'S NOTES
The development, preparation, and publication of this work has been undertaken with great care.
However, the Publisher, employees, editors, and agents of The Haworth Press are not responsible
for any errors contained herein or for consequences that may ensue from use of materials or information contained in this work. The Haworth Press is committed to the dissemination of ideas and
information according to the highest standards of intellectual freedom and the free exchange of
ideas. Statements made and opinions expressed in this publication do not necessarily reflect the
views of the Publisher, Directors, management, or staff of The Haworth Press, Inc., or an en-
dorsement by them.

This is a work of fiction. Names, characters, places, and incidents either are the products of the
author's imagination or are used fictitiously, and any resemblance to actual persons, living or
dead, business establishments, events, or locales is entirely coincidental.

Cover design by Kerry E. Mack.

Library of Congress Cataloging-in-Publication Data

Schwartz, Helen Ruth.
    The meadowlark sings / Helen Ruth Schwartz.
        p. cm.
    ISBN-13: 978-1-56023-575-0 (pbk. : alk. paper)
    ISBN-10: 1-56023-575-6 (pbk. : alk. paper)
    1. Gays—Fiction. 2. Exiles—Fiction. 3. Lesbians—Fiction. 4. United States—Politics and
government—21st century—Fiction. 5. Feminist fiction. I. Title.

PS3619.C4867M43 2006
813'.6—dc22

                                                                            2005029137

This book is dedicated to those committed
to equal rights for lesbians and gay men.

Editor's Foreword

Alice Street Editions provides a voice for established as well as up-coming lesbian writers, reflecting the diversity of lesbian interests, ethnicities, ages, and class. This cutting-edge series of novels, memoirs, and nonfiction writing welcomes the opportunity to present controversial views, explore multicultural ideas, encourage debate, and inspire creativity from a variety of lesbian perspectives. Through enlightening, illuminating, and provocative writing, Alice Street Editions can make a significant contribution to the visibility and accessibility of lesbian writing and bring lesbian-focused writing to a wider audience. Recognizing our own desires and ideas in print is life sustaining, acknowledging the reality of who we are, as well as our place in the world, individually and collectivity.

Judith P. Stelboum
Editor in Chief
Alice Street Editions

Prologue

⟿◈⟿

They say it began with the gay rights march on April 25, 2010, when one million people gathered before the Department of Justice Building in the District of Columbia to demand equal rights and fair treatment for gays, lesbians, and bisexuals in the United States.

The right-wing religionists, seeing the event as an opportunity to increase their flock and fatten their coffers, preyed on the fears of middle-class America by suggesting that the march was the beginning of a homosexual takeover of the United States. "It's a sad day, indeed," said Patrick Olmstead of the First People's Ministry, "when nude queers with whips and chains line the streets of our nation's capital and proclaim the right to rule America." Pictures of three topless women and one man in leather shorts with handcuffs in his pocket were repeatedly shown on right-wing television stations, convincing viewers that these were the leaders of the "depraved" march.

In little more than three months, Olmstead's sentiments were being echoed throughout the country by a generation of Americans who were so tired of economic chaos and unemployment that they were willing to believe anything in order to have an enemy to rage against. By the end of 2013, homosexuals had become the enemy. The march, instead of becoming a source of strength for gays, became a rallying symbol for heterosexuals who began to openly preach discrimination and violence.

In 2016 and 2017, twelve states passed legislation that encouraged discrimination against homosexuals. Sodomy laws went back on the books. Gay bashing became common. The president of the United States, who had aligned himself with homosexual rights during his campaign, retreated from his earlier position and chose to ignore the evil that was festering.

doi:10.1300/5559_01

1

The situation catapulted in 2017, when *First Person* magazine put Patrick Olmstead on the cover as the best-loved man in America. Gay gathering places and organizations began to disappear. Homosexuals became the majority on the unemployment lines. And the violence increased. Lynn Bremmer, one of the topless women who appeared on television during the gay rights march, was found dead on the steps of the Lincoln Memorial in Washington, DC. A handwritten sign left next to her body said, "Kill the Queers!" Her murderers were never found.

By 2018, the situation was completely out of control. But then something happened that changed the focus of public attention. On June 30 of that year, the great earthquake, predicted for decades, hit California. It began with a rumbling virtually ignored by Californians. It ended with 32,000 dead, 180,000 injured, 4,000 missing, billions of dollars of property damage, and a new island.

As the earthquake traveled up the state of California, approximately forty miles east of the coast line, it created a chasm that quickly filled with the raging waters from the Pacific Ocean. Killing or destroying everything that lay in its path, the ocean split off a land area approximately 40 miles wide by 720 miles long, separated from the mainland of America by ten miles at its narrowest and eighteen miles at its widest points.

Fearful that the aftershocks would wreak further havoc on the involuntary residents, the military and national guard evacuated the island within twenty-four hours after its creation. There were no people left to put out the fires that were allowed to rage out of control. Mud slides and flooding destroyed what the fires didn't get, and within three weeks, there was nothing visible but a billboard that said, "Patrick Olmstead for President," considered a "sign from God" by members of his growing flock.

For almost one year, the island remained untouched while Americans recovered from the effects of the quake. When the island finally became the topic of conversation, public discussion confirmed that nobody wanted to inhabit it; its future was too precarious. Scientists could not guarantee that the unstable environment would not cause the strip of land to further divide. "It will be gobbled up by the sea" was the favorite prediction of solemn geologists.

Such was the atmosphere of the country when John Robb, president of the Gay Rights Coalition, met with the president of the United States. Theirs was not a public meeting. It was conducted in great secrecy and privacy, and might not have been conducted at all had John not been the president's closest political advisor and confidant in earlier years. It was a meeting the president owed him, and John took full advantage of the debt.

"Mr. President," he began, "we live in a time of great evil. For too long, too many remained silent and allowed the right-wing religionists to establish a foothold in this country, a foothold that is threatening to destroy the constituency that I represent. Sometime, in the not-too-distant future, Patrick Olmstead will come to power, and a holocaust will occur. As a man of compassion, I ask you to take a role in its prevention."

By the end of the historic meeting, several major decisions affecting gays were made, chief among them the granting of the new island off the west coast to the Gay Rights Coalition for habitation by homosexuals. All homosexuals would be given the opportunity to relocate to the island by 2022. Those homosexuals who chose not to leave the United States would be subject to the same laws that governed gays in the military; they could march in parades and go to gay bars but could not engage in homosexual conduct, including kissing or holding hands. Persons remaining in the United States who disobeyed the gay gag laws would be subject to arrest and a lengthy jail sentence.

To make sure that all homosexuals were made aware of their options (and their sexuality), the government, spurred on by Patrick Olmstead, began a series of DNA-chromosome testing. All persons who tested positive for the Scarpetti gene, named after the physician who discovered it as an indicator of homosexuality, were encouraged to emigrate. Parents of minors made the choices for their "gay gene" children.

It was decided that after the year 2022, no choices were to be made. All newborns would automatically be tested for the Scarpetti gene.

Those testing positive would be transferred to the island prior to their third birthday.

Contrary to expectations, many homosexuals accepted with joy the opportunity to relocate. Almost all chose to leave the United States. On May 12 of the year 2020, the first day of the exodus, the one million deportees included seven senators, fourteen members of the House of Representatives, the leader of the Democratic Party, eighty-three professional athletes, a bevy of millionaires (who were allowed to take their money with them), and 1,400 members of the entertainment industry, including Ray Breyer, America's heartthrob.

Encouraged by the beginning of the exodus, the number of emigrants quadrupled by the end of the first year and included one justice of the U.S. Supreme Court, a member of the president's cabinet, three more senators, the wife of the attorney general, the country's leading tennis player, and Ellyn Hargreaves, the woman billed as the world's greatest blues singer.

By the end of the second year, the number of departing drained America's military forces, necessitating the reinstatement of the draft; the court system was left in chaos by the absence of judges; the National Football League was forced to cancel the 2022 season; and the emigrants joked that America was on the verge of requesting financial aid from the new island.

Such was the beginning of Cali, the nation of homosexuals.

One

⸻⸙⸻

Cara tried to suppress a smile as she turned to leave, but she could feel the corners of her lips twitch plaintively, almost demandingly. *Damn,* she cautioned herself, *one little grin and you'll blow the professional image that got you this assignment in the first place.* She clenched her right hand—which was out of view—into a fist, pressing the balls of her fingers against the fleshy part of her palms, hoping to distract herself from her emotions.

"It's okay to smile, Cara. Enthusiasm and spontaneity are two of the reasons why you were selected for this job," said the prime minister, as if reading her mind. "Don't disappoint me by acting like any other stuffy bureaucrat." Placing her elbows on her desk, chin resting on entwined hands, the prime minister awaited the reaction of Cali's youngest cabinet member.

"Yes!" Cara threw her hands in the air with customary gusto. Turning to look at the woman who had just given her the assignment she had coveted, she bowed in good-natured fashion. "Thank you, Madam Prime Minister. Thank you." With a grin as wide as her elation, she exited from the office.

Prime Minister Miriam Ekstrom watched the door close before she allowed herself the pleasure of a chuckle. She adored Cara. Her energy and eagerness reminded the PM of herself when she was young. Her grace, of Barbra. With a forlorn glance at the photo that always stood alone on the corner of her desk, Miriam got up and walked to the windows that overlooked Cali. It was said that the prime minister's office in the Lynn Bremmer Building had the most beautiful views on the island, a fact undisputed by its occupant. Before her stretched the valleys and hills that led to the western edge of the Pacific, the bright green foliage of young plantings contrasting sharply with the deep

doi:10.1300/5559_02

hues of the ocean. But it was not at the west window that Miriam stopped. She continued to the south window, gazing at the hills that had once been the Pacific Palisades.

Thirty-seven years ago, in the year 2018, Miriam had lived in those hills, in one of the magnificent houses that dotted the landscape, sitting one atop the other until they crested on the flatness of the pinnacle. Her view then, no less beautiful than now, was a special part of the life she had shared with Barbra.

The PM blanketed her arms about her chest, warding off the cool breezes that rolled in off the Pacific, remembering, as she did, the unseasonably cold air on June 30, 2018, the day that her life began to fall apart.

"What's going on?" Barbra had asked when Miriam returned to their Washington, DC, apartment early. "Has your meeting been cancelled?" Standing at the kitchen counter, eyes fixed in concentration, she turned her back to Miriam and began smoothing the delicate yellow frosting on the carrot cake.

Oh, my God, thought Miriam, leaning against the refrigerator, her ear pressed against the soft humming noises. *She hasn't heard yet.*

"Well, what's wrong? It's not like you to come home in the middle of the day." Alarmed by Miriam's silence, Barbra started to shake. "Why aren't you answering?" She untied her apron and threw it on top of the counter. Turning to face Miriam, her voice exploded. "Are you sick? Tell me what's happened!"

Leading her pregnant lover to the living room, Miriam sat her down on the couch and tightly grasped her hand. She opened her mouth to speak, but words wouldn't come.

"Talk to me. You have to tell me," Barbra's scared face begged.

"The president was called away before the meeting began. California was hit by an earthquake," she said softly, eyes cast down, scanning the invisible weave on the beige rug.

"How bad?"

The answer came in slow metered words. "Bad. Worse than anything we ever expected. A major portion of California is totally destroyed. Thousands are dead. Thousands more dying. A part of the state broke off and is separated from the rest by a chasm of water." She continued with her eyes focused elsewhere, avoiding the anguish on her lover's ashen face. "California, as we know it, no longer exists."

"No! No! I . . . I can't believe it—" were the only distinguishable words Barbra emitted. The rest was guttural gibberish. Senator Miriam Ekstrom wrapped her arms around her lover and tenderly rocked her while darkness descended.

All night they watched television. Scene after scene, portrayed in shocked silence, affirmed the devastation. The Pacific Palisades, their home for six years, was nowhere to be seen. Gone. Simply gone. With most of their family and friends.

"It's okay. Everything will be okay," Miriam exclaimed with a resolve she didn't feel. Cupping Barbra's tear-stained face in her hands, she stated resolutely, "We're going to be all right. You, my love, are going to have a healthy baby girl. We are going to be okay." She kissed Barbra's tears as they merged with her own.

For the next eighteen months, they were okay. Then part two of their tragedy was played. In preparation for the homosexual exodus to the new Pacific island, mandatory genetic testing of all U.S. citizens began. Miriam and Barbra tested positive for the gay gene. Sixteen-month-old Cheryl tested negative. As they both knew, heterosexuals were not permitted to emigrate to the island.

For two months, they argued about leaving the United States, Miriam begging Barbra to leave Cheryl in the care of her doting grandmother. "You and I cannot stay," she insisted. "We are documented homosexuals. Scarpetti-gene positive. As soon as Patrick Olmstead comes to power, that information will be made public and I will be voted out of office." Consumed by the determination to persuade Barbra, Miriam portended the bleak future. "Once my sexual orientation is made known, our lives here will be a living hell. Cheryl will be taken from us. We will—"

"They cannot take my daughter," screamed Barbra, banging her fist on the dining room table.

"They can, and they will! Barbra honey, listen to me." She picked up the pamphlet she had received in the mail from the Gay Rights Coalition and began reading. "If you choose to remain in the United States, then you must refrain from all homosexual activities. Should you kiss a person of the same sex or even be suspected of kissing a person of the same sex," she paused for emphasis, looking at Barbra, "you will be subject to interrogation and a jail sentence of indefinite determination. Effective the day you become documented as being Scarpetti-gene positive, you have no civil rights. The bastards in power can actually lock the door and throw away the key." Miriam laid the pamphlet on the table and left the apartment. When she returned two hours later, Barbra and Cheryl were both gone.

The note was simple:

> I love you. I will always love you. Your freedom must suffice for us both. Cherish it, and do not look back.

Three months later, after an exhaustive search turned up no leads about Barbra or her daughter, Miriam Ekstrom became the first United States senator to join the exodus for Cali. Twenty-four years later, she became Cali's first lesbian prime minister. But she continued to look back.

Shaking with the rage of her memories, the prime minister took several short, deep breaths before closing the windows and returning to her desk.

Once again resuming her role as Cali's leader, she called her press secretary and told him to announce Cara's special assignment.

Two

Upon leaving the prime minister's vestibule and reaching the anonymous comfort of the hall, Cara surrendered the last vestiges of professional decorum. She half ran and half skipped to her own office one floor below, paying little attention to the quizzical expressions of those she passed.

"What is going on?" demanded Esther, her secretary, as Cara bolted through the door. "I've received several calls asking if you were going to hold a press conference and one call from a man," she hastily grabbed a piece of scrap paper from the middle of her desk, documents flying everywhere, "named Tim Felmar, who said he was going to be your escort officer. Where are you going? Where is he escorting you to? And wherever it is, keep in mind that you can't go without me." She jumped up from behind her desk and ran after Cara who had continued skipping directly into her office.

"I've never seen you quite like this before. What's going on?"

Jumping to a seated position atop her desk, Cara spoke quickly, a characteristic tendency when excited. "The PM just informed me that I got the New York assignment. I am going to New York City, USA . . . as Cali's official representative to the World Conference on the Aging. Tim Felmar, the escort officer, will be going with me. I am actually going. It will be the first time in eight years that a Calian has visited the United States and that Calian is going to be . . ." Pausing for emphasis, she declared in a bellowing voice "Cara Romero." She held both hands to her face in a gesture of genuine delight, jumped off her desk, grabbed Esther around the waist, and led her across the floor in a mock jig. "I can't believe it. I really can't believe it. I can't process this." Flushed with excitement, Cara leaned against the wall, gasping

doi:10.1300/5559_03

deeply. "Well, aren't you going to say something? Say something! What do you think?"

"I think you need to spend some more time at the gym before you go anywhere." Esther looked pleased with her response. At sixty-six, physical exercise had become one of her two primary obsessions. Dominique ice cream baked with caramel glaze was her unfortunate second.

"Oh, come on, Esther. Tell me how happy you are for me."

The older woman took Cara's hands in her own, gently patting them, almost caressing them. "You know how happy I am for you. No one deserves this assignment more."

Few people would have argued that point. At thirty-two, Cara was one of the most respected leaders of the Calian government, achieving her status with many friends and almost no enemies. Her climb to the top began with a bachelor's degree in geriatrics, followed by a master's in political science. Then came the rungs on the ladder of government. She bruised no egos and stepped on no feet as she performed each job with characteristic enthusiasm and proficiency, garnering the respect of young and old alike. It wasn't long before she reached her highest rung to date as Director of the Office for the Aging, a cabinet-level position. And now, adding spice to her future, she had just been handed the prestigious assignment as representative to the World Conference on the Aging, a meeting being held in the country of her birth.

For a Calian, a visit to the United States was a coveted honor, available only to those at the highest levels of government. Because of America's efforts to keep bearers of the Scarpetti gene from mingling with the country's pure strain of heterosexuals, the United States granted visas only to those foreigners whose passports were stamped Scarpetti-gene negative, unless, of course, their entry was government sanctioned. Inasmuch as Cali and the United States had no diplomatic relations, official visits were rare. Few Calians had ever had the opportunity to visit the home of their parents, almost no Calian at all since 2047—the year of the beating of Brian Rayford, Cali's minster of agriculture, in Washington, DC.

Brian, attending a meeting of the World Council on Hunger, was clubbed unmercifully in front of the Washington Monument by a group that preached the doctrine of hate formulated during Patrick Olmstead's administration. Although Olmstead had died shortly after his first term as president, these ragtag disciples, dubbed "Olms" by the press, devotedly followed his tenets and relished harassing, and occasionally beating, those gays who chose to remain in the United States during the great exodus.

Although the Olms' violence against American homosexuals was largely ignored, the beating of Brian, a guest from Cali, was considered a particularly despicable act by America's citizenry. After all, two of them, and none knew who, were his parents. Their consciences stirred, Americans sentenced the assailants to long jail sentences, angrily disrupted Olm meetings, and set fire to the DC warehouse that stored their posters and handbills. The mindless oppression of the Olms was broken. Although they remained a political force, the raw power of undisputed violence had been refined.

But that did not soften the heart of Miriam Ekstrom. Outraged by the violence committed against a citizen of Cali, the prime minister refused to allow a Calian to participate in any conferences conducted in the United States. Until now.

"How come we are attending the Conference on the Aging?" an amazed Cara had asked the prime minister upon being informed of her designation as Cali's representative. "Has the policy on Cali participation in U.S. conferences been changed?"

"No. Not really. This is simply the first one in eight years covering information that we are interested in sharing," Ms. Ekstrom had responded, eyes twinkling in surprise at the boldness of the young woman's question.

"Esther," said Cara, returning to her present thoughts, "I really am very honored. I hope—whoops, there goes your phone, which should start ringing off the hook about now. The PM was releasing the information as I left her office. There will be no formal press conferences. With less than two weeks to departure, there's much too much to do. Refer all media personnel to the prime minister's press secretary. Call Tim Felmar and tell him I'll call him tomorrow. Oh God, I guess the

THE MEADOWLARK SINGS

first thing I had better do is call my mothers. I don't want them to hear this from the tube."

Moving to her desk chair, Cara allowed herself a few moments of private smiling time and then pulled the phone from her pocket, requesting immediate access to her mothers' visual. She knew it would be Sue who would answer—it almost always was—and that was the mother to whom she really wanted to speak. New York had been the senior mother's home for her first twenty years. The exodus had been difficult for those her age, who, as adults, had been forced to leave family and friends rather than live under the restrictive gay gag laws. For Sue, it had also meant giving up medical school and ambitions she conceived in childhood. Her bitterness never quite dissipated. Although Sue and Donna enjoyed a good life in Cali, had been granted Cara, and held responsible positions with the government, an element of anger permeated her life. It was an element common to Calians past the age of fifty.

When Cara's image appeared on the telephone screen in the living room, Donna was lying on the couch with a half-read newspaper. The timer showed four minutes allotted for pickup, more than enough time for Sue to answer.

"Won't you even talk to your own daughter?" asked Sue as she raced into the room. She had just finished showering after spending the morning fertilizing the vegetable garden. Dark wet hair peeked from under a terry cloth turban. A bath towel hung around her neck.

"I'd rather just sit here and watch her." Staring at the life-size monitor from her recliner, Donna put the newspaper aside and watched Cara sort through the papers on her desk, her eyes frequently glancing at the flickering light of the telephone. "Look at her, Sue. I know she's not ours biologically, but somehow, there has to be a connection."

"Why do you say that?"

"She's beautiful." Donna grinned. "That long sun-washed blonde hair, it's just like my mother's. Mom even wore it that way . . . loose, just long and loose, in waves down to her shoulders. Her blue eyes. They're your father's. Soft neon blue. Talkative. Those eyes speak. And they smile. Just look at the way they smile. She's excited about something. Can't you tell?" Donna walked up to the screen and outlined Cara's face as she turned to speak to Esther who dropped some documents into the red box. "The shape of her face. That's your father's too. Crisp angles without harshness. And those wonderful pale freckles that belonged to your mother. They lend such warmth to her soft cheekbones. And just watch her, Sue. Watch the way she uses her beauty. Turns her head at just the right angles. Plays her eyes like an instrument. All that, she must have gotten from you."

"And what, pray tell, did she get from you?"

"Her tall, slim lines. Assertiveness. And her radiance, of course."

"Yeah, right." Sue chuckled, playfully swatting at Donna with the bath towel as she reached up and pressed the visual button. "You're on, Cara. Excuse my robe. I'm just out of the shower."

"That's okay. I'm glad I got you both." Cara peered into her mini desk screen, adjusting the volume. "Good news and I want to make sure you hear it from me first. The prime minister just announced that I'll be Cali's representative at the World Conference on the Aging in New York City next month." She spoke quickly, trying to deny her mothers their objections. "I can barely believe it. You are talking to the woman who is going to be the first Calian to visit the United States in eight years."

"I'm not sure that makes me happy." Sue cast an annoyed eye at Donna who was smiling in approval.

"Come on Mom, please be happy for me. It's a wonderful opportunity. Nothing bad is going to happen. Tim Felmar—he has an excellent reputation—is going with me as the escort officer, so I'll be well protected."

"Felmar?" Donna interrupted. "His lover, Glen, is my secretary. He didn't say a word about this."

"This is probably the first secret the governing council has ever kept," muttered Sue. "Cara, I'm sure this must mean a great deal to you, and I can't stop you from attending, but I want you to know that I don't approve. New York is a dangerous place. It's not like Cali. It doesn't even resemble Cali. It's like no place you've ever been."

"That's exactly why I want to go."

"Spoken just like mother Sue's daughter." Chuckling mischievously, Donna bent down and picked up the bath towel that had fallen to the floor, kissing the back of Sue's neck as she draped it around her shoulders.

They spoke for a few more minutes, Cara promising to spend the weekend with them before abruptly ending the conversation in order to take another phone call. She hesitated before pressing the response button. The call did not come in on the visual mode, but the return number that now blinked across the screen was the most familiar one in her collection. It was Jody's.

"Are you in or out?" asked Esther's voice on the intercom. "And you'd better make a quick decision. The way the phone is ringing, I don't have a lot of time to wait on you."

"Well, okay, I'll take it. Jody may be just what I need to bring me back down to reality." Still, she sat for another few moments staring at the receiver. Twice she reached for the audio button. Twice she pulled her hand back. Finally, after pushing her own visual switch to off, she took a deep breath and turned on the speaker.

She began. "I see news really travels fast when you're a member of the prime minister's inner circle."

Surprised by the uncharacteristic sarcasm, Jody hesitated before responding, "Catty, catty, catty." Nervously, she paced the room. This was not going to be an easy conversation. She was glad she had not turned on the visual. "That's not like you, Cara. Besides, I didn't hear it from the PM. It's been announced on the news. You're all over the tube. Cara Romero is going to New York City as the Calian representative to the World Conference on the Aging. You have to be deaf, dumb, and blind not to have heard it."

"Sorry. That was rude of me. I apologize. So, how have you been?" Just the sound of Jody's voice was enough to crimp her good humor. *Oh well,* she thought. *Maybe Jody is the karma to keep me from outgrowing humble.*

"Fine. I've been fine. Say, maybe we ought to get this out in the open right now. Margo may be the PM's daughter, but that doesn't give me access to privileged information. As far as the PM is concerned, when it comes to government, I'm like any other Calian."

Irritated by her own defensive reaction to Jody's call, Cara began stumbling over her words. "Look, it's been eight months since we've spoken. I don't understand. Why are you calling? I'm sure it's not to say congratulations. And you said everything else you had to say to me eight months ago when you chastised me for my long list of imperfections. Or did you miss something?"

Jody felt the anger rise in her cheeks. "Now wait a minute. Let's be fair. You're the one who wanted out. You're the one who didn't want a committed relationship. I wanted you. And you know it. You voted to end our relationship. Why are you so angry at me? Is it because I found someone else? Is that why Cara? Because I'm happy?"

Yes. No. I don't know, thought Cara. In a self-nurturing gesture, she ran her fingers through the shock of hair that fell across her forehead and spoke again. "I'm sorry. Really sorry. Maybe the upcoming trip has made me a little more tense than usual. I just learned about it a few hours ago and I haven't quite absorbed it all yet."

"That's fair." There was a long pause before Jody continued, "I'm not sure whether I should even ask this now, but the reason I was calling was to see if you would join me for dinner before you leave for New York. Tomorrow night, perhaps, or sometime over the weekend? Is it possible?" Considering the way the conversation had begun, Jody flinched, expecting an unequivocal no.

"Yes, it's possible. It might even be nice, but the weekend is out. I promised my mothers that I would spend it with them. Let me look at my schedule for tomorrow." Cara knew her calendar was open, but she needed a few minutes to compose herself. She lowered her voice to a normal range and inhaled deeply. "Tomorrow is good. You name the time and place."

"Topanga's at eight." Tension relieved, Jody sat down and began doodling on the computer screen. "And it will just be the two of us. Margo won't be coming."

"I assumed that. I don't know that I'm quite ready to meet her, so it's just as well. Topanga's at eight. See you then." Just before hanging up, she quickly added, "And Jody, I really am sorry. I'll try to clean up my behavior before tomorrow."

Cara pressed the termination button, leaned back, and put her feet up on the desk. She stared at the vacant phone monitor, beckoning it to give her some answers. *What the hell was that all about?* she wondered. *I was angry, really angry. And Jody is absolutely right—if I had agreed to a commitment ceremony, she never would have looked for anyone else. I refused. And now I'm angry. Is it because she's with someone else? That doesn't make sense. What's going on?* She sat and mused over the problem for the better part of an hour. *Maybe I'm just lonely,* she decided. *Maybe it's simply time for a new relationship.*

Three

Cara tried to enter Topanga's unnoticed, but that was an impossibility for the popular member of Cali's cabinet. Table after table jumped up to greet her, some with handshakes, others with hugs. Most people had already heard the news and there were calls of congratulations and spurts of applause.

Good heavens, thought Jody. *It's like watching the wave at the sports arena.* People rose and sat, rose and sat. And Jody stood among them and patiently waited for Cara to reach the table, attentively studying the body that fashion designers loved to dress. Long and sensuous with legs that wouldn't quit. And Cara knew how to flatter them—with flowing silk pants that began at the hip line and ended grazing the floor. What Jody didn't know, of course, was how many hours Cara had spent selecting tonight's wardrobe. She had been in and out of her closet all day, picking and discarding until she was satisfied. She had finally chosen the light blue silk blouse with the darker blue pinstripe silk pants.

"On you, hip-huggers look superfluous," said Jody as she reached the table. Cara paused for a moment, warmly looking at the woman whose body had given her so much pleasure over the years. It was just a moment, but long enough to convey the affection she was feeling.

Hugging Jody with a familiar exuberance, she spoke in her usual high-spirited fashion, forgetting her resolve to remain aloof. "I've missed you. Oh, how I've missed you." She extended her arms, holding the attractive woman by the shoulders and searching her face. "You look wonderful. Margo must be very good for you."

Jody smiled in the self-conscious manner that Cara always elicited and nodded. "Yes, she is. She's a good person. A very special woman." She brushed back her auburn hair and awkwardly waited for Cara to

doi:10.1300/5559_04

sit, not quite sure whether the etiquette they had established during their three years together was still in effect. But Cara didn't hesitate, and Jody relaxed as she continued the conversation. "But I've missed you too. It was good seeing you walk in that door. It was—I don't know—just natural." She paused to take the menu from the waiter. "I'm starved. I'd like to order before we talk if that's okay with you."

Cara studied Jody as she read the menu and was surprised by the warm flush of her own reaction. She was absolutely adorable. Not beautiful. Maybe not even very pretty. But adorable! The soft auburn hair curled around the gamine, almost waiflike face with the sparkling brown eyes—wonderful, expressive eyes that were almost too large for the delicate balance of features. And those incredible lips. Full, soft lips. Kissable lips. *So lovely,* thought Cara. *If only she had been less jealous, less controlling, more the soft person of her appearance and less the adversarial creation of her legal training. If only I had been able to be the person she wanted. If only I had been less independent, less driven—*

Jody interrupted her thoughts. "I'm going to have the angel hair pasta with goat cheese and sun-dried tomatoes."

"Soft tacos with Brie and wild mushrooms for me. Iced tea. And bottled water for both of us." Cara smiled at the waiter, then turned to face Jody. Placing her elbows on the table, she leaned forward, not speaking until the waiter moved on to the next party. "Now you must tell me what this dinner is really about." Reaching for the switch, she flicked on the aromatic mist that sat in the triangular recess in the center of the table. "Almost like old times." She smiled.

"Why don't we enjoy our meal first, business later?" Jody leaned across with crinkled nose and squinted eyes and sniffed the sweet odor. "Cinnamon. The verdict is cinnamon."

"Spoken like the attorney I've known and loved," said Cara, as they put up their hands and high-fived.

"Sincerely said. Sincerely taken." Jody laughed.

Anyone watching the two women dine would have thought they were lovers. There was something about the way they inclined their heads when they spoke, the familiar manner with which Jody reached over and tasted food from Cara's plate, the lowering of eyes as they exchanged smiles of intimacy. Even their behaviors complemented each other. Cara, so animated and energetic, her speech punctuated by her body's gestures. In contrast, Jody was reserved and dignified. She sat erect and still, only her eyes giving expression to her speech. In actuality, their behavior emulated each other's appearance.

"I've had it," said Jody when she finished the main course. "I can't eat another thing, but don't let that stop you from enjoying dessert."

"Nothing ever stops me from enjoying dessert." Cara ordered two hazelnut coffees and Topanga's famous seven layer chocolate cake, tilted her chair, and stretched her legs under the table. Finding Jody's foot, she tapped it with her own and asked in a deliberately plaintive voice, "Now, isn't it time yet? I'm having a perfectly wonderful evening, but aren't you ever going to tell me why we're having this reunion?"

Jody leaned forward, placing her forearms on the table. Cocking her head to one side in the "I'm getting serious" mannerism with which Cara was familiar, she spoke hesitantly. "There is something I want you to do for me when you're in New York."

Cara sat up straighter in her chair, apprehensive about what was to follow. She knew Jody well enough to know that this would not be an easy request to fill.

"I want you to try to contact an American woman named Barbra. She is an older woman, in her early sixties—"

Cara cut her off, almost angry. "It's against the law for me to make personal contacts. You know that."

Jody reached across the table and covered Cara's hand with her own, a characteristic gesture that meant "just listen." "Hear me out on this. It's important. Barbra is not just anybody. She is the prime minister's lover."

"You mean she *was* the prime minister's lover."

"No. I mean she *is*."

"Come again?" Cara removed her hand from under Jody's and sat erect in her chair, looking at her with an incredulous expression. "You'd better give me some details on this."

"'Was' would have been correct at one time." Providing as much detail as she knew, she related the story of the women's relationship prior to the exodus from the United States in the year 2022. Waiting for a reaction, she paused and ordered another cup of coffee. "Hotter than the first," she called to the waiter.

"We're still on 'was.' I must be missing something. How did it become 'is'? How is it possible for a Calian to be involved in a love affair with an American citizen?"

"In 2047," continued Jody, "Brian Rayford, Cali's representative to the World Council on Hunger, was badly beaten on the streets of Washington, DC. Private physicians were afraid to treat the gay man. Dr. Barbra Weissman, a documented homosexual working for the United States government in California, was called in."

"How did she become a physician?"

"After the exodus to Cali there was a serious shortage of doctors in the United States. The government offered free tuition and subsidized living to those willing to work for the federal government after the completion of medical training. Barbra qualified for the program because health care personnel were needed to work in the area of homosexual testing and deportation."

"That's incredible. Go on." Cara sat on the edge of her chair, fascinated with the story.

"When Brian returned, he told the prime minister all that he knew about the woman who had treated him, including the fact that Barbra was assigned to the California homosexual embarkation program. She worked with Cali's health personnel and was responsible for assuring that the infants placed aboard the exodus ship, the *Fantasia*, were in good health prior to leaving the United States for the trip to Cali. Barbra conducted physical examinations of the children on Wednesdays and Sundays in the onboard clinic at the port in Pasadena, California." Jody paused to finish her second cup of coffee. "You can probably guess the rest."

"The PM's days off were on Wednesdays and Sundays until a few weeks ago." Cara stood up and shook her head in disbelief. "That's an incredible story. Absolutely incredible." She turned to look around the restaurant and realized they were among the few people still seated. "Please finish."

"That's the problem. There really is no finish. Two months ago, Barbra did not appear at the clinic. She has not been seen since. The

Fantasia staff, sworn to priority secrecy by Ekstrom, have been trying to learn her whereabouts. It's rumored that she's been transferred to a job in New York City, but nobody knows for sure."

"And that's where I come in." Walking up behind Jody, she placed her hands lightly on her shoulders. "Does the PM know that you're telling me this story?"

"Ekstrom doesn't even know that I know. I heard it from Margo. The PM was afraid that something might happen to her in the United States so she told Margo the entire story several years ago. Margo told me right after your assignment was announced."

Tenderly massaging Jody's neck, Cara waited a few moments before speaking. "Ah, some things never change. That muscle is still the barometer of your tension." Walking back to her seat, she sat down and leaned toward Jody, speaking in the soft hush of the conspirator. "I'll do what I can, but I don't know exactly what I can do. Let's leave it at 'I'll try.'"

"That's all I'm asking," said Jody, taking a position that was the mirror image of Cara's. When they were almost nose to nose, Cara bent her head and gently kissed her on the lips.

"You know something . . ." she murmured as she pulled her head away. "At this moment, I really envy Margo."

"Just remember, you had your chance," Jody said with a grin as she watched Cara signal the waiter for the check. Changing to a more somber expression, she looked directly into the eyes of the woman across the table. "I really loved you. In some ways, I'll always love you. Whatever it is you're looking for, I hope you find it. And when you do, I hope it's everything you want it to be."

"Sincerely said. Sincerely taken." Cara smiled.

It was past midnight before the two friends left Topanga's.

Four

The weekend was a disappointment for Cara. She had not spent time at the home of her parents for several weeks and had actually looked forward to the visit. But the joy of a reunion was overshadowed by Sue's strong opposition to the New York trip.

"She can't turn it down. It's an honor. Be reasonable," Donna kept saying.

"She can turn it down. It's dangerous. The whole assignment should be cancelled. No one should have to go to New York."

"I can't refuse to go," Cara intervened, punctuating each word with insistence. "So the two of you may as well stop arguing. I'm going. That's a definite. Tim Felmar is an excellent escort officer. Gary Kane begins the briefing program tomorrow. Everything has been arranged. This is not an issue for debate, and that's not why I'm here. I'm here because I love you and wanted to spend some time with you before leaving." She wrapped both mothers in her arms and hugged them tightly.

Still, the arguing continued.

On Saturday afternoon, Cara got a break. Sue and Donna, laden with gifts, went off to visit friends whose first grandchild had arrived from the United States the week before. Cara, delighted to have the time alone, decided to spend the day at the lake that meandered in the valley behind the house.

With picnic basket in hand, she made her way down the winding private path, now overgrown with shrubs, vines, and lack of use. But even five years later, since her last visit to this nurturing spot, the memories were poignant as familiar odors of childhood hovered lightly in the air. Although the dock was smaller than she remembered and partially shaded by trees that she couldn't remember at all,

doi:10.1300/5559_05

it was still her dock, still the first place she had kissed another woman, still the first place she had cried when she learned that Sue and Donna were not her biological mothers.

Setting her basket down, she rejoiced in the beauty of the resplendent day. The sun in its zenith sent down streams of smog-free light, emblazoning the landscape with its warmth. Refreshing westerly breezes cooled it off.

Cara removed her shoes and socks and sat on the dock with her feet dangling in the water. Making ripples with her toes, she watched the widening circles fan out to the opposite shore. Across the placid waters, she could hear the giggles of excitement from young Michael James as Jonathan, his new father, taught him how to fish. "When ya see the bobber go down, Mikey, ya gotta pull up real fast. That's the way ya gotta do it so ya don't lose the fish that's on the other end. Know what I mean, Mikey?" Cara heard the plunk of a bobber breaking the glistening flatness. Then minutes of silence. "That's it! That's it! Hey Beau! Beau! Mikey got a fish." Cara heard the voices fade into the distance and was pleased with the hush that descended.

After eating the hastily made sandwich of tuna fish and sprouts, she spread the oversized beach towel on the dock and stretched out on her back, wondering how she had ever thought the plastic dock boards comfortable. How could she have possibly made love to anyone on this dock?

Tuning her watch to soft music, she closed her eyes and listened to the wind as it agitated the leaves, rustling softly, and she thought about Jody and the previous night's dinner, a wonderful encounter. Without hurting each other they had wordlessly conveyed their feelings of mutual adoration while declaring their independence. As Cara read it, the evening had been a closure to their restless and unsatisfying relationship as lovers and the opening to their future, and, hopefully, harmonious relationship as friends. She was grateful for the transition. Because of her high position in government, good friends were a rare treasure. She needed friends. And now that the status of their relationship had been put in perspective and redefined, perhaps Cara could get on with the task of "falling in love."

Her thoughts turned to the upcoming assignment. It was the most exciting of her blossoming career. And she knew that representing Cali in the United States would inflate her resumé with the potential of even greater responsibilities. Although Cara was good at her job and displayed a comfortable amount of confidence for one so young, she had feared that her career path in human services would eliminate her as a choice for an international appointment. Those assignments were normally reserved for political aspirants whose careers involved diplomatic relations. But she had gotten the nomination. *All things are possible,* she thought, as she turned on to her stomach, stretching languidly in the warmth of the sun. *And, if all things are possible, I may be able to find Miriam Ekstrom's vanished lover. Hell, I may even be able to find my own lover.*

Awaking several hours later, she returned to the house in time to greet her returning mothers. An afternoon that began with greetings and smiles gradually turned to arguing once again, Sue steadfast in her determination to persuade Cara not to leave Cali. "I just know something bad is going to happen, and Felmar's black belt in judo is not going to protect you. In New York, a submachine gun would not be enough," she persisted.

By Sunday morning, Cara decided to cut her visit short, preferring the solitude of her apartment and the company of her cat to the bickering of her mothers. Hugging the diminutive Sue tightly as she left, she said with conviction, "Trust me! Everything is going to be fine. Nothing bad is going to happen."

"I'd feel better if you weren't so damn naive. You don't know anything about men," muttered Sue to herself as she walked back into the house.

In the background, Donna shrugged her shoulders.

Five

Arriving early on Wednesday for the first day of briefings, Tim Felmar waited patiently. Never having met Cara Romero before, he wanted to impress her with his reliability. Although he had not been with the diplomatic corps when Brian Rayford was attacked eight years earlier, he realized that the failure of the escort officer to protect Brian had damaged the small organization, causing a loss of confidence. Tim wanted this trip to be perfect, and he wanted Cara to know it would be perfect before they ever left Cali. Her trust and faith were essential to their success.

"You're gorgeous! A New Yorker will never believe you're a lesbian, Ms. Romero." Tim smiled as Cara walked up and introduced herself.

"Maybe I'll just tell them I'm a gay man," she quipped as they shook hands. "And please call me Cara." Very tall, dark curly hair, small dark penetrating eyes, broad shouldered, probably of Italian heritage, she had recognized him from the description as soon as she entered the room.

"And a sense of humor too. This may be one of my better trips." He led her to a table to await the arrival of Gary Kane, the government's briefing officer. After a few minutes of polite conversation, they became silent, taking in the activities surrounding them in the cavernous hall that sat next to Cali's wharf.

They were sitting in the enormous greeting area of the harbor's homosexual disembarkation section. It was an oversized room filled with rows of folding chairs reserved for the adoptive parents of children arriving from the United States. Although the *Fantasia* had just pulled in and the youngsters would not be brought ashore for several hours, anxious couples had already started gathering. They flowed in

doi:10.1300/5559_06

through the multiple sets of doors that had opened only one hour earlier. Some sat; others paced. They spoke in small groups, sharing their excitement. Laughter swept through the room in a domino pattern, illustrating the infectious joy that was spreading. *This is a happy place,* thought Cara. She wondered about those parents in the United States who had just surrendered their lesbian and gay children who had tested positive for the Scarpetti gene. What emotions must they be feeling?

"This is one briefing I wouldn't have missed for the world," said Tim as he surveyed the festive scene. "My lover, Glen, and I have applied for parenthood. We hope to be sitting in this waiting room before 2055 is up."

"I see you've already met." Gary Kane, looking very much the bureaucrat in his three-piece brown suit, shook the hands of both Cara and Tim. "I'm sorry I'm late. A last-minute meeting with the PM delayed me. Why don't we start the tour right away, then we can return to my office and begin the actual briefing." He turned to Cara. "I'm not quite sure why you wanted to observe the immigration program. Is there something special in which you're interested?"

Yes, there was. She was interested in learning more about the last known workplace of Miriam Ekstrom's lover. "No, nothing special," she answered, trying to sound sincere. "I just think we should be familiar with the procedures that occur on board the *Fantasia.* I'm sure it's an area of concern to Americans and I'd like to be able to answer any questions they may ask."

In fact, Cara wasn't at all sure that there was any value in touring the ship. Inasmuch as Barbra was no longer affiliated with this aspect of the homosexual deportation program, the tour was probably a waste of time. But, then again, it might give her some inside knowledge that would be helpful in finding the vanished physician.

"Well, okay. Let's begin." Gary turned and signaled them to follow. Exiting the noisy room, the threesome walked toward the gangplank that led aboard the *Fantasia,* the ship that brought America's homosexual children to Cali. Cara felt an elation surge through her body and shared an involuntary smile with Tim. "We were here once," she said softly.

At the end of the gangplank stood Emily Wagner. One look at her face and it was evident that she had no desire to escort VIPs through her domain. Emily was a no-nonsense lady who, as the administrator of the *Fantasia,* was totally devoted to her job and the children. She had no lovers. No other interests. The *Fantasia* had been her life since its inception thirty-three years earlier. Visitors she regarded as intruders. Except for the prime minister. Emily adored Miriam Ekstrom, and because Ekstrom had interceded and asked permission for Cara's group to board the ship, she would try to be polite, a characteristic not normally attributed to her.

After the obligatory exchange of greetings and introductions, Wagner led her visitors through the maze of corridors to the board room where, with the use of diagrams and wall maps, she explained the ship's organizational structure.

The *Fantasia,* they learned, boarded in Pasadena, California, at 5:00 a.m. on Wednesday and Sunday for the ten mile voyage to Cali. Approximately 3,500 children up to the age of three years old arrived each day. Boarding was by government authorization only, each child having been registered for deportation by the hospital in which they tested positive for the Scarpetti gene. After registration, the infants were permitted to remain with their biological parents only until their third birthday. Forcible transfer to Cali occurred after that date. Once on board the *Fantasia,* they were divided into one of four holding areas. Section One was for newborns under six weeks. Two was for disabled children. Three was a miniature hospital for those suffering an acute illness or needing onboard medical attention. Section Four, the main area, housed children who did not fit into the other three categories. Adult emigrants—Scarpetti-gene positives born before 2022 who did not leave the United States during the great exodus—assisted staff members.

"Why do we accept sick children?" asked Tim when Wagner had put down the pointer.

"If we did not, some of these children would never get well. Their biological American mothers would keep them sick to avoid giving them up. You would do the same thing if it was your child." She turned her back, indicating that she would not entertain any more questions and said simply, "Follow me," which they all did.

As Gary pushed open the doors to Section Four, the largest section and the first to which they were escorted, Cara braced herself, expecting to be overwhelmed by the noise of children crying and screaming, but the room was eerily quiet.

"Hypnotic tranquilizers," said Wagner, pointing to the ceiling. Looking up, they saw pale green diaphanous images floating by in slow rhythm to the haunting melody of a harpsichord. The images dipped and swayed, doing a ghostly minuet against the black background of the surrounding walls. "It's a special blend of sight and sound that has a sedative effect in combination with the rolling of the ship. Do not look; it can affect adults as well."

Forcing her eyes from the magnetic attraction, Cara looked down the length of the ship. Row upon row of cheerfully painted cribs were being tended by hundreds of lavender-uniformed staff members. Infants and young children in pink or blue buntings were being hugged, held, caressed, massaged, fed, diapered. She was awed by the sight.

"I've never seen so many children." Tim tiptoed up to a crib, reached in and with his large hands gently stroked the cheek of a gurgling infant. His smile broadened when the child gripped his index finger. "I could really get into this."

"This room holds up to four thousand individual cribs. Crib assignments are made as soon as the children are brought aboard. The records of each child are then placed in the attached storage pouch." Reaching into the closest crib, she pulled out some official-looking documents. Scanning them, she reviewed the information aloud. "This two-year-old child was born to parents of average height and weight who were thirty-eight and thirty-three when the baby was delivered. The biological parents are of Jewish descent and were born in the USA. Three grandparents, ranging in age from sixty-nine to seventy-six, are still alive; the fourth died in an accident two years ago. Five great-grandparents are alive and in good health. They range in age from one hundred one to one hundred eight. Of the three who are deceased, two died in the 2018 earthquake and one died of heart disease at the age of eighty. The maternal great-grandmother was diagnosed with diabetes at the age of ninety-one. The child has no known allergies, no distinguishing marks, and tested positive for the Scarpetti gene three weeks after birth."

"I'm impressed." Cara reached into the adjoining crib and picked up a yawning baby, eyes scrunched shut, she judged to be under one year. "The records are really much more thorough than they were when I was brought to Cali." Broadly smiling, she held the baby to her chest and gently patted her on the back, waiting for Wagner to reprimand her. "Is this allowed?" she finally asked when no admonishment was forthcoming.

"Yes. We encourage touching. We have no records of how much love these children received from their heterosexual parents." She reached into a bright yellow crib and ever so gently with precious care and a delicate touch, lifted a tiny boy with big blue eyes and porcupine black hair. Sweetly, she cooed, grinning as the child responded with gurgles and smiles. She kissed his pudgy cheeks and nuzzled his stomach with her nose. Giggling, he pulled her hair with his chubby fingers. She threw back her head and laughed with him, crooning softly as she did, "Ga, ga. Oooh, coo, coo, coo." Eyebrows raised, Tim and Cara exchanged bewildered looks, surprised at the tenderness being displayed by a woman they had labeled a scrooge. *So much for her austere trappings,* thought Tim. Carefully placing the baby back in the crib, she began walking to the far end of the room. "Follow me."

As they walked down the aisle, the three visitors oohed and aahed, touched babies, and smiled at staff members who were quietly moving from one child to another. They stopped only once when Cara, thinking there had been a mistake, said with urgency, "There are two little girls in that crib."

Wagner nodded to one of the female staff members who responded in a singsong voice normally reserved for infants. "Yes, that's deliberate. They are identical twins. The two little girls are siblings, sisters who were produced from one fertilized egg. We frequently get identical twins with both having the Scarpetti gene. That's not the case with fraternal twins. It's unusual for fraternal twins, derived from two separate eggs, to both have the Scarpetti gene. Sadly, this little boy in the next crib is one half of a set of twins. He has the Scarpetti gene.

His brother, who remained in the United States, did not." Lifting the child, she held him up for the visitors to see. "But we'll give him plenty of love to make up for his loss." Then, inexplicably, she began to lose her grip on the baby who emitted a startled cry. The group watched in horror as Cara reached out, caught the child in midair and fell down with the tiny boy safely in her arms.

Apologizing profusely, the attendant took the crying baby while the rest of the group clustered around Cara, helping her to her feet. "It's a good thing I was a softball player." She laughed, but she began to wince as soon as she tried to put weight on her left foot.

"Are you all right?" Gary looked at her with concern.

"Damn. I think I sprained my left ankle."

Emily Wagner, flustered by the event, began to nervously wring her hands. "This is terrible. I'm so sorry. Let me get you to the hospital clinic where one of our doctors can check and make sure nothing is broken."

Cara swore silently. *I wanted to see the hospital, but not this way.* Her ankle was beginning to swell and the pain was excruciating. *This had better not affect the New York trip,* she thought.

Brought by wheelchair to Section Three, Cara sat in the examining room awaiting the arrival of the ship's physician. "I'm sorry, it's going to be a little while," explained the attendant Wagner had sent with her. "Dr. Wiese is in the clinic covering tattoos. The children have already been anesthetized so he can't take a break right now."

"I don't understand. What do you mean 'covering tattoos'?"

The attendant began to stammer, wondering whether she had given out too much information. Deciding that she had not violated any policies or priority secrets, she continued. "Some of the babies have been tattooed by their biological parents with United States phone numbers or addresses. If we find a tattoo during physical examinations, it's surgically covered. It's not a major problem. Only about fifty children on a normal day. But it does take a bit of time. The doctor should be done in a half hour or so."

Adjusting the ice pack Wagner had given her, she winced before speaking. "That's an awful thing to do to a child. Where do they tattoo them?"

"Anywhere. Behind the ear. In the genital area. Even between the toes. But fifty children a trip isn't bad. Thirty years ago, it was more than one thousand. When we put out the word that we cover the tattoos aboard the ship, the number dropped. Actually, what we do is laser the area with a grafting patch so the child is left with a nice neat scar. It doesn't deform." She lifted her long hair and turned her back to Cara. "Look at the base of my neck. That's what it looks like when Wiese gets done."

Cara stared at the two-inch long rectangular area, several shades lighter in color than the surrounding skin. Looking like a tiny Band-Aid, it was identical to the soft patch that she had so lovingly kissed on the inside of Jody's thigh.

Sitting down on the doctor's stool, the attendant nervously folded and unfolded her hands. The stool squeaked in rhythm with the rocking of the ship. After a few minutes, she began tapping her foot impatiently. "Say, would you mind if I left you waiting by yourself? I've got some kids I haven't fed yet and I'm kind of anxious to get back to them."

"No, not at all," responded Cara, pleased that she would have some time alone in the examining room.

After the attendant left, she looked around the small room. Except for the lime green color, it was like any other doctor's office that she had ever visited. Diagnostic equipment hung on the walls over cabinets that were probably filled with more examining tools. A small sink. No windows. Sparse furniture. A table for the patient. The swivel stool for the physician. A desk. And a single bed. Although she could guess what the PM and Barbra used it for, she wondered what its real purpose might be. Probably for the use of ill staff members or adult emigrants, she concluded. Her eyes riveted to the bed. She wondered what it must have been like for the two women to have sex after a pause of twenty-seven years.

It was seven years ago, on the third visit to Barbra aboard the *Fantasia,* that the PM decided to take the initiative. Walking up behind

Barbra, who was rambling on about her life in California while returning examining equipment to the cabinets, she kissed the back of her neck, her lips lightly brushing the wisps of hair that curled at the nape. Placing her hands on her shoulders, she gently turned her so they were facing one another. She put her finger to Barbra's lips. "No more talk. It's time. I want to make love to you."

A barely audible moan escaped from the petite physician who nervously ran her fingers through her graying hair. "I don't know. It's been so long."

"All the more reason why we shouldn't wait any longer," Miriam responded. She took Barbra's hand and led her to the bed, sitting while she left Barbra standing in front of her. "Please," she said. "Let me remove your clothes. My eyes want to see what they have missed these twenty-seven years." She reached up and with a scarcely visible quiver, she unbuttoned the front of Barbra's white uniform, slowly, button after button. She did not hesitate. The dress fell gently to the floor, exposing her body in sequential layers—her shoulders, her unrestrained pale breasts, the small waist, and the silk panties that Miriam had loved to touch. She wrapped her arms around her waist, pulling her forward while pressing her cheek gently against the unblemished firm breasts yet unaffected by aging. The familiar scent of Chanel wafted to her nostrils. "I've waited twenty-seven years to hold you again," she whispered as she breathed in the aroma and felt the nipple hardening against her cheek. She took the left nipple in her mouth, sucking and feeling it ripen with her tongue. As Barbra groaned, she moved her lips to the other breast, grazing it gently. She lowered her head to Barbra's panties and rubbed against the softness of the material that covered her throbbing lover. With one motion, she moved her hand, pulling at the elastic, guiding the silk to the floor. "Oh," she murmured as she gazed at the still graceful body, "my eyes have missed much." Gently, she pulled Barbra on to the bed and positioned her along its length. Then she stood and removed her own clothes, never removing her eyes from Barbra's thirsting gaze. "You are my heart," whispered Barbra as the PM laid down beside her. Undeterred by age, urged by the rocking motion of the ship, the two women engaged in the acrobatics of lovemaking as though a delay of twenty-seven years had never occurred.

Lost in thought, Cara almost didn't hear Dr. Wiese when he entered the examining room. "Okay, let's take a look at that ankle." She grimaced as he lifted her foot and inserted it into a scan box. Watching the image portrayed on the wall screen, he pointed to the area that was causing the greatest pain. "You're lucky. No breaks. A slight sprain. Some pain for a few days. Can be controlled with aspirin. Try to keep it elevated and you should be fine in a few weeks. Any questions?" He turned his back before she had the chance to respond.

Hobbling only slightly with the tightly bandaged ankle, a relieved Cara caught up with her tour group as they were about to leave Section One. Nodding to her cohorts, she tried to ignore the sounds assaulting her ears. Screams and cries and giggles all mingled. Conversation was impossible in this, the newborn, area. Of course, thought Cara, infants are not affected by visual images. Hypnosis did not work here.

"So, am I going to escort you or will you have to be replaced by some beautiful young man?" Tim asked Cara with twinkling eyes as they returned to *Fantasia*'s boardroom.

"Sorry," interjected Gary, "my job won't permit a New York trip. You'll just have to take someone else."

"Okay, you guys. Don't even tease. I'm leaving on schedule. My gait may be a little more awkward, but it's going to get me there. A sprained ankle is all it is."

In the boardroom, Wagner again indicated that she would not answer any questions. She had kept her agreement with the PM and personally escorted the young bureaucrats on a tour of the *Fantasia*. There was no reason to prolong their visit. Besides, she was anxious to return to her children. She left them at the gangplank.

With little time left in the day, the group decided to call it quits, planning to reassemble at Gary's office the following morning to begin the formal briefing program.

Six

⁃≺∾⧣∽≻⁃

"What a drag," moaned Tim during their Monday coffee break. "I can't believe the utter boredom of the whole thing. If I knew I'd have to go through this, I would have refused escort duties outside of Cali."

In the days that had passed since their return from the *Fantasia,* they had endured six-hour classroom sessions each morning, followed by lunch and a return to their regular jobs for the afternoon. For Cara that meant going down one flight of stairs to the Cali Office for the Aging. For Tim, however, it meant traveling by light plane to the University of the South where he was assigned part-time as a professor of international relations.

Cara, who had never heard a murmur of complaint from Tim, was surprised by his reaction and bewildered by his statement. "You mean you've never been out of country?" she asked with a sinking feeling.

"I scared you, didn't I?" responded a startled Tim. "Not to worry. I've traveled outside of Cali four times. Stateside, to New York, twice. A long time ago. On diplomatic missions. Never as an escort. So these briefings are all new to me. I guess diplomats aren't required to know as much stuff as escorts."

Cara too was overwhelmed by the amount of material they were covering. Six hours had been devoted to the historical relationship between the United States and Cali, with most of the attention given to the religious right's condemnations of homosexuality. The next six hours covered rules of protocol in the United States and at the conference. Stateside fashion and customs was the subject of this third day.

Immediately following their coffee break, Gary Kane accompanied them to a simulated American clothing store for the acquisition of attire appropriate to New York. Because of the varying American atti-

doi:10.1300/5559_07

tudes toward homosexuality, it was considered imperative that they blend with the general populace and not be identified as Calians. Repulsed by their new clothing, Tim and Cara continued to complain.

"These clothes have no style at all," groaned Tim as he looked in the mirror. "The colors are drab and the materials are boring. If Glen saw me in these every day, there would be cause for divorce. And," he added, "I couldn't blame him."

Wearing a plain, light brown dress with a high collar and awkwardly puffed sleeves, little pearlized buttons to the waist, Cara sighed. "I spend twenty hours a week in the gym developing my muscles and then the Americans want me to hide them. My constituency at the Office for the Aging wouldn't wear this! I guess I don't have to worry about being cruised by New York women. Or men for that matter. It's amazing, Calian clothes have so much more style."

They were right, of course. During the great exodus, some of the world's most famous fashion designers had emigrated to Cali and the stylish design schools they established were among the most popular in the country. Innovative clothing developed. New synthetics, replacing the raw materials destroyed during the earthquake, attracted the attention of the fashion minded. They were light and textured, appealing to the tactile as well as the visual. Colors were vibrant and diffused through layers of transparencies, creating new colors in the same way dawn and dusk altered the sky, and in a bold new experiment, some Calian clothes were being treated with perfumes, creating a banquet for the senses.

Gary Kane, whose own bureaucratic three-piece outfits resembled the old-fashioned American clothes they were modeling, displayed little sympathy for his students. "These unattractive, uninspired outfits you so detest may keep you from getting killed by the Olms on this trip. Think about that tomorrow when we cover crime in the United States."

"Whoops," whispered Tim, "I think we hit a nerve."

"Think so," Cara agreed as she entered the dressing room to change back to her state-of-the-art outfit.

Seven

⏤⯑⯑⏤

It was the next day when Cara decided to tell Tim about Barbra.

They were sitting in the Robb restaurant of the Lynn Bremmer Building, having a casual lunch and discussing the morning's session. Animatedly, she used her hands as exclamation points as they reviewed the material she had found so shocking. "What scares me about New York is the crime." She leafed through her training manual and quoted the numbers directly from its pages. "In one week in July 2052, fifty-eight people were murdered; and on one day in June 2053—just one day—" she emphasized, looking up at Tim, "fifteen were killed. That's horrendous. Fifteen murders are more than we have in Cali in a year. And rape! Rape is almost unheard of here. And the old followers of Olmstead, the Olms, they're the scariest of all." She looked over and winked at the four young women sitting a few tables away who had been gawking at her during lunch. Giggling, they lowered their eyes to their plates. "Damn, I'm so bad. I had better remember not to do that in the United States, or I'll become another statistic for this training manual."

"Just keep in mind that in New York, it's the men who do the winking at women. Especially at attractive, blonde, thirty-two-year-old women."

"Not at this woman they won't. Not in the clothes I'm going to be wearing. Besides, I'm going to cling to you like mud clings to a pig."

"In that case," asked Tim, slapping at a fly that was buzzing around his salad, "would you mind wearing Glen's perfume?"

"Only if you wear Jody's."

After the laughter faded, Tim cleared his throat and assumed a more serious expression. "So, there is someone in your life. I had wondered if there was anyone." He waited for her response.

doi:10.1300/5559_08

"Not anymore." She sighed. "Jody was an important part of my life for three years. Last year, she announced that she wanted a commitment ceremony. I announced that I didn't. I adored Jody; actually, I still do, but not enough to surrender my single status. Monogamy is not my thing. She is now with Margo and happy. I am now single and miserable. I am also very, very monogamous."

"Well, I guess we'll just have to change that," said Tim slapping his hand on the table. "I bet there are a lot of women out there who would love to have Cara Romero in their bed. Should we forge ahead with introductions or is there still a possibility of a reconciliation with Jody?" Noticing a spot on his pants where he had apparently sprayed salad oil while futilely swatting at the fly, he dipped his napkin in water and tried to remove it. With exasperation, he finally threw down the napkin and reached for the stain remover wipes kept in little packets near the salt and pepper. "These newfangled things really work," he said with amazement as the splotch slowly faded into the fiber.

Cara gazed out the window at the Pacific, losing herself in the rhythm of the spray as it flew off the waves. She could almost feel herself being absorbed by the panorama that swept before her. Her mind became blank, a state she was able to summon when confronted by problems with which she was not ready to deal. She referred to it as meditation; Jody had called it blocking. Self-nurturing, she ran her hand through her hair.

"Hello. Is anybody home?"

Startled, she turned her head and faced Tim. "Sorry, my mind ran away with itself. What was it you asked?"

"Any chance of a reconciliation between you and Jody?" he repeated as he toyed with the wrapper from the packet.

"No. I used to think there was, but no, not anymore." Cara paused to take a deep breath. *I'm saying things aloud that I've just barely discovered,* she thought. "Jody is happy with Margo. They're good together. We weren't. We spent most of our time arguing. Two assertive women really don't make for a good relationship. Add ambition to the equation and you have two women who are better off as friends. I think we'll stay friends."

"My apologies. I didn't mean to pry or bring back any unpleasant memories."

"Actually, the memories you brought back were very pleasant. Maybe that's the problem. I haven't quite let go of them yet."

As she paused to organize her thoughts, the four young women at whom she had winked tentatively approached the table. "Ms. Romero," began the tallest one who was being pushed from behind by the other three, "we just want you to know that we're very proud of you. We think it's wonderful that you were chosen for the New York assignment and we want to wish you good luck."

After Cara had graciously thanked them and the women had left the dining room, she again turned her attention to Tim. "Not to change the subject, but I'm glad they wished us good luck. Luck is something we're going to need."

"Oh, is there something you haven't told me?"

"As a matter of fact, there is." And she proceeded to tell him the story about Barbra and the prime minister. He did not interrupt, but sat quietly and listened, nodding or frowning occasionally as she spun out the details. Finally, when she had finished, he raised both hands playfully and his resonant voice echoed her thoughts. "Hallelujah! I knew there had to be a good reason why that great lady is single. When we get to New York, we're going to find this Dr. Barbra, tie her up with a lavender ribbon, kidnap her, and bring her back as a gift for the PM." Despite his large size, Tim suddenly looked very much like a little boy. A cute, mischievous little boy.

"Thank you. I kind of knew you would feel that way." Slowly, with measured deliberation, she took a long swallow of coffee. Casting her eyes down, reluctant to look at him, she again spoke. "But, I must tell you, this really isn't a simple matter. You know, contacting Barbra is illegal."

"So is homosexuality in America, and being they've made it almost impossible for me to break that law, I guess I'm going to have to teach them a lesson and break this one." She loved the way he smiled. His face lit up, the dark eyes sparkled, and the dimples deepened. "I have a feeling," he continued, "that finding Dr. Barbra is going to be a lot easier than you think. Probably easier than finding you a new lover."

Quietly, Cara sat finishing her coffee. The thought of doing something illegal was unnatural for her. In thirty-two years, she had been a model citizen, never having knowingly broken a law. Could she do this? she wondered. Would she actually attempt to contact an American? Then she thought about the prime minister. By meeting Barbra on the *Fantasia*, particularly at a port in the United States, she had actually been engaging in an illegal act for years. Somehow, she had difficulty identifying Miriam Ekstrom as a criminal.

After returning to the briefing room, they were pleased to learn that they would not have to endure any more classroom days. In an effort to confuse the American media, already hyping the arrival of the homosexuals from Cali, the travel plans had been changed. They would be leaving three days ahead of schedule—the next morning.

Before leaving the Bremmer Building they were summoned to the office of the prime minister. Miriam Ekstrom was standing with her back to them, looking out the south window, when they entered. Turning, she nodded to the two chairs in the middle of the room and resumed her seat behind the massive plastic desk.

"So," she began, "you have been briefed and now you know all that there is to know about the United States and your assignment." She paused and when there was no response, she continued. "It must be very exciting for you to be going off to the land of your biological parents, but I want you to know that it is we who are your real family, who will be thinking about you and watching your progress with great interest. As the navigator of your career," she looked directly at Cara, "I will be watching you with particular interest."

Squirming self-consciously in her seat, Cara grimaced as she tried to cross her ankles, her left still swollen from the sprain. "Thank you," she repeated after Tim.

"Oh, Cara, forgive me for not mentioning this sooner. I was very pleased to learn of your athletic prowess aboard the *Fantasia* the other day. If not for you, that child could have been very badly injured. How is your ankle?"

This woman knows everything, thought Cara silently. "It won't affect the trip. Thank you for asking, Ms. Ekstrom," she responded. Placing her feet side by side, she vowed to sit still.

"Good, but that's not the question I asked. Let me repeat. How is your ankle?" Miriam was surprised at her own bad-mannered response. Embarrassing a subordinate was not characteristic of her. *My irritability has something to do with the United States and Barbra,* she theorized.

For the briefest moment Cara felt her eyes water like those of a reprimanded child, but quickly she regained her composure. "My ankle is much better. I'm walking with only a slight limp. And the discomfort is barely noticeable."

"Good, I'm glad to hear that." Turning to face Tim, she asked, "And how is Glen?" She didn't wait for an answer. "I understand that the two of you had already applied to be parents, so the visit aboard the *Fantasia* must have been of particular interest."

"Glèn is fine. Yes ma'am, we have applied and we're very excited about it. Actually, since my visit aboard the *Fantasia,* we've been thinking about changing the application to twins."

While the prime minister exchanged pleasantries with Tim, Cara glanced around the office. It was, she thought, an appropriate reflection of Miriam Ekstrom. It was a strong office, decorated in bold colors. Deep blues, maroons, and browns. No delicate pastels for this woman. The heavy plastic furniture, so much in style in this country without forests, was placed hither and yon. Conversational chair groupings were not in evidence. Looking at the marbleized plastic desktop, her eyes were drawn to the lonely framed photograph of the light-haired young woman that sat in the upper corner, angled so it could be seen by visitors and the PM. *The devil is making me do this,* Cara thought. Pointing, she said in a voice designed for Tim's ears, "What a wonderful photograph. Is that you, Ms. Ekstrom?"

"No," said the PM succinctly. She continued the conversation as though the question had never been asked. "And what about you, Cara, do you plan to adopt children?"

Bingo, thought Cara. *That's Barbra.* Seeing a photo of the real person strengthened the kinship she was feeling with the American woman. Looking at the prime minister, she answered the question with no hesitation. "Not yet. I think I'd better find a mate first." She wondered whether the PM knew about her past relationship with

Jody. Probably, she did. Her familiarity with the backgrounds of her staff members was legendary.

Suddenly, as though remembering another appointment, the prime minister stood, signaling the end of the meeting. *That was quick,* thought Tim, *the fastest interview I've ever had with Ekstrom.* "Well, I'd better let you attend to your packing and last-minute arrangements," the PM said as she walked them to the door. "I want to wish you both the best of luck. This is our first effort in eight years to improve relations with the United States. I'm counting on the two of you to make it meaningful. Have a successful trip. Be proud of who you are and the country you represent." She shook Tim's hand, and turned to Cara, saying, almost as an afterthought, "I'd like to see you privately for just a moment."

Returning to the office, she did not sit, nor invite Cara to sit. Standing awkwardly, Cara tried not to shift weight to her left foot as she waited for the prime minister to speak.

"You and I," the PM finally began, "have worked together well these past several years. In addition to being a top administrator, you are an excellent advocate for the aging. Some of the programs you have introduced represent great progress in the way we relate to our older citizens. You have been chosen for this assignment because you earned it." Motioning Cara not to interrupt, she walked to the south window and sat on the ledge. "But you are also very young. And very beautiful. American men will have great difficulty accepting your homosexuality. Be careful. You must carry yourself with pride, dignity, and a small measure of aloofness. Be polite, but be the consummate professional. Most important, do not let them mistake your enthusiasm for romantic ardor." She stopped briefly to observe Cara's reaction. "Always remember, men from other countries are heterosexual and they will view you as a love object. You cannot relax in the safety of a dispassionate relationship the way you can with Calian men," she finally concluded.

A blush slowly crept up Cara's neck until it covered her entire face. *Crimson,* she thought. *I must be crimson.* Ignoring the pain in her ankle, she restlessly rocked back and forth, praying that the PM would not start telling her about the birds and the bees. Her discomfort was especially severe because of the high esteem in which she held Miriam Ekstrom. Her reverence for the woman had once bordered on a child-like infatuation which her secretary, Esther, teasingly referred to as a crush. Being spoken to this way by her idol produced an embarrass-ment of great intensity.

"Yes," she stammered, rubbing her hands together with nervous energy. She felt little beads of perspiration forming on her forehead. "I will be very careful. I'll keep a lot of distance between me and the men. Thank you for speaking to me about such personal matters."

"Why Cara," she responded, "I do believe you're embarrassed. Well, don't worry about it. I feel about you as I do my daughter, and these things need to be discussed."

Cara smiled bashfully. The PM smiled knowingly. The two women parted after warmly shaking hands, Miriam Ekstrom laughing to her-self as she closed her office door. *I guess this old girl can still get a rise from the younger set,* she thought proudly.

Eight

Anisette, alternately meowing and purring, trailed Cara as she walked from room to room. "How do you always know when I'm leaving?" she asked aloud, bending to scratch the calico's ears. "I don't even have the travel bags out yet and already you're yelling at me. Now listen," she said as she sat in an armchair and Anisette jumped into her lap, "Vanessa is going to take very good care of you while I'm gone. She's going to feed you all your favorite fish dishes, play with you, and give you catnip treats. You're going to be a very spoiled kitty by the time I get home. What am I talking about? You're already spoiled." She started to get up to begin packing, but sat down again as the cat began kneading her arm. "Okay, okay, I'll make my phone calls instead."

Her first call was to her neighbor, Vanessa, to let her know that she'd be leaving early the next day. "Remember, this cat is my child," she said repeatedly.

"If you say that once more," chided Vanessa, "I'll have you committed to a home for the mentally ill."

After speaking to her mothers and again trying to assuage Sue's fears, she decided to call Esther. Although she had seen her secretary in the office earlier that afternoon, their meetings the past few weeks had been brief and she wanted to have a little more contact with her before she left.

"Hey, Marge," she began when the image of Esther's lover appeared on the screen, "Cara here. You know, I haven't spoken to you in a long time. I'm glad you answered. It gives us a chance to say hello. How are things?"

"Good. Good. Essie, it's Cara," she yelled, sticking her head out the kitchen door into the hall. "Everything's fine. Look, I'm pleased you

doi:10.1300/5559_09

called. It gives me a chance to wish you good luck in New York. Essie is a bit out of joint, but I'm very excited for you." As usual, Marge barely paused for a breath, chattering away nonstop. "I'm really pleased that she's not going with you. I'd worry the entire time the two of you were gone. This way, I only have to worry about one person. Know what I mean? Look, don't forget that as soon as you get back we want to have you over for dinner. How about that, I said 'don't forget' as though you'd already been invited. I think I forgot to invite you. Well, it doesn't really matter. You are invited. I told Essie I'd make you your angel hair pasta dish. So plan on it. Oh, here comes your favorite secretary now. Let me put her on."

"Any problems, Cara?" Esther asked when she took the phone.

"No, none at all. I just wanted to review some of the things that may come up while I'm in New York. And I wanted to give a few minutes of special attention to my favorite secretary."

"Thank you. That makes me feel better."

"Esther, I'm sorry. I didn't realize you were upset. Until Marge just said something about you being out of joint I didn't have a clue that anything was wrong. Now tell me, what's bothering you?" She was surprised when Esther turned off the visual.

"Look, I don't know how to say this, but I'm really hurt. I've always traveled with you as an escort until now." Cara sensed Esther's pain as she visualized tears welling in the eyes of the robust woman with the moon-shaped face. "It's as though the PM thinks I'm good enough to escort you in Cali, but not good enough for New York. It's not right."

Damn, thought Cara. *What an insensitive jerk I am. If I had made an effort to spend more time with her these past two weeks, I would have known she was hurting.* "But it has nothing to do with your qualifications Esther. It has to do with your sex. The powers that be thought it would be better if I was escorted by a man, lest the Americans think that Cali's homosexuals travel with their lovers." She paused, waiting for her to mull over the information. "With Tim, there can be no questions about our relationship and our status as representatives. Oh Esther, I'm sorry. I should have explained this to you right away."

There was a long pause. "I never thought of that. Of course. It makes perfect sense," she exclaimed, taking a deep breath. "Oh, I really must apologize to you. I thought maybe you said something to the PM about not wanting me to go with you. Maybe I was getting too old for the job. Maybe I was being put out to pasture. I should have known better than to think such things of you. I feel like a fool."

Cara breathed a sigh of relief. In Cali, where people bonded closely with co-workers in the shared absence of an abundance of relatives, she had developed a particularly close relationship with Esther. Repairing the crack in their friendship was important.

"Don't worry about it. I'm the one to blame for your confusion. If I had explained things to you immediately, you wouldn't have spent the past two weeks agonizing. Or feeling rejected. I'm the one who owes apologies."

"Hey, you know something?" interjected Esther. "I'm really kind of flattered that someone might think I was your lover. Wait until I tell Marge that one."

After a good-natured chuckle, they got down to work and discussed some of the things that might come up in Cara's absence. The conversation ended much more pleasantly than it had begun, with each woman vowing to be more up front with the other in the future. "Our relationship as co-workers and friends means a great deal to me. Let's not mess it up with a failure to communicate," beseeched Cara as she ended the conversation.

She remained sitting for a long time after hanging up, berating herself for her insensitivity. Neglecting to explain to Esther why Tim had gotten the assignment was inexcusable. Cara had never been a thoughtless person. Quite the contrary. She had always been an individual who cared a great deal about the feelings of the people she loved. *Maybe I'm just overwhelmed with this assignment,* she thought, *or maybe I'm getting too big for my britches and need to put things in better perspective.*

Placing a meowing Anisette gently on the floor, she walked into the kitchen, pressed a few buttons on the cookery machine, and awaited the preparation of her food. Although 7:00 p.m. was an early dinner hour for her, she wasn't quite ready to begin the arduous task of packing. After eating a leisurely meal of sesame chicken and noodles, commenting aloud on how good they were making home-cooked foods lately, and reading the evening newspaper, she found herself pacing again, almost tripping over a sleeping Anisette who had finally settled down in her favorite spot near the armchair. "I just know I'm going to kill myself tripping over you one of these days," she mumbled.

Sitting in the armchair once again, she stroked the cat, who allowed it with sleepy indifference, and thought about how much she enjoyed her apartment. In crowded Cali, where space was a premium, Cara had the good fortune of occupying a corner two-bedroom apartment overlooking the Pacific. The living room, framed by a wall of glass, offered incredible views on two sides. But it was the master bedroom that was her special joy. Lovemaking in the surround-stereo bed augmented by the sounds and sights of the ocean made for superlative orgasms. Vanessa teasingly referred to it as "the best fuck room in the west."

Watching the sun set over the ocean, she turned on the phone with vague deliberation. Although Jody had not been one of the people she had originally planned to call, she found herself dialing the confidential number with a comfortable familiarity. To her delight, the conversation was much warmer than she had anticipated. Warmer and more relaxed.

"Here, take my international phone number with you," Jody volunteered. "Don't hesitate to call should you need me or my legal advice. Remember, these may be our parents, but some of them hate lesbians."

"How did you get an international phone number?" Cara asked.

"I'm an advisor to the Prime Minister on international law," she responded, quickly adding, "I got the appointment before I met Margo."

"I wasn't going to say anything."

"Like hell you weren't. Don't forget, I'm here if you need me."

After completing the phone calls, she began packing. It was a task made more difficult by the fact that she hated almost every article of clothing she was taking. *I'm not going to a fashion show,* she reminded herself with annoyance. Then she had problems deciding what other things she needed in New York. Did she need to bring a hair dryer or would New York hotels have built-in hair dryers? How about her electric toothbrush? Did she need to bring the base charger or just the brush? It was too late to call anybody to check. Finally, she decided to just take whatever she might possibly need. At 1:00 a.m., she removed a complaining Anisette from her travel bags, zipped them shut, showered, and climbed into bed next to the cat.

Sleep did not come easily that night. Nightmares became dreams and became nightmares and became dreams. The prime minister laughed at her. The woman in the photograph on the PM's desk, waving with both hands, transformed into Mother Sue while in the background, Esther kept yelling, "I told you so. I told you so." Tim, with identical twin boys sitting on his shoulders, kept zipping and unzipping her bags, a laser patch visible on the back of his arm. She floated in and out of a restless state, turned the soft sleep music on and off, listened to the rain and the raging ocean, and moved a purring Anisette off her head and on to the adjoining pillow. Finally, she surrendered to the alarm clock at 7:00 a.m. and groggily got out of bed to begin the preparations for putting on her American clothes.

Nine

The plane left Cali Airport in the early afternoon for the two-hour ultrasonic jet trip to New York City. As the only passengers, Cara and Tim had the luxury of the spacious airliner to themselves. Immediately upon boarding, he began reading the *New York Journal,* which had been placed on their seats while she went into the VIP lounge and stretched out on the air bed. Grateful that they had been scheduled for the two-hour ultrasonic G-1 flight rather than the half-hour G-2, Cara decided to try to get in a short nap. Pressing her watch for a pulse check, however, she realized that her excitement level was much too high for sleep and she sat up and opened her briefing papers instead.

Although her role at the conference had not yet been confirmed, it was anticipated that Cara would be presenting research documents attesting to the success of Cali's care facilities for the elderly.

Begun in the early 2020s, Cali's state-of-the-art program of facilities for the aged had been the work of Miri Mills, Cara's predecessor, who in 2018 had been the head of the Bureau of Nursing Home Affairs in the United States. On the day that Miri learned she had the Scarpetti gene, she unhesitatingly applied for transfer to Cali, although it was affectionately rumored that Miri would have applied for transfer even if she had tested negative. The opportunity of establishing an elderly health care program from scratch was more meaningful for her than sex.

As Cali's new director of the Office for the Aging, the first thing the tiny woman did—even before Cali had a constitution—was legislate that the new country's facilities for the aged could be established only in association with universities. The rest was easy.

doi:10.1300/5559_10

At each university it became a mandatory part of the curriculum for students in health and human services to spend four hours weekly in the affiliated nursing home, guaranteeing that each elderly patient had his or her share of direct contact with young adults. At almost any time of the day, there was a ratio of seven or eight people under the age of twenty-five for every one person over the age of eighty-five.

But Miri didn't stop there. To keep Cali's seniors interested in contemporary affairs, she also mandated that the university establish a theater for its drama students in affiliation with the adjoining elder care facility. Because the theater also served as a meeting place and auditorium for the surrounding community, Cali's nursing home patients continued to attend political meetings and lectures as well as cultural presentations. Some even joined theater groups or worked as ushers and ticket takers.

The third part of Miri's three-pronged approach was the more difficult to administer, but produced the most meaningful results. A nursery for immigrant children became the architectural focal point of the nursing home—university complex. In it were housed the newly arrived children for whom adoptive parents had not yet been selected. These were the youngsters who entered the country unexpectedly early, their emigration records lost in the maze of U.S. bureaucratic procedures.

The nursery, centrally located and most often attached to the university at one end and the nursing home at its other, served multiple purposes in Miri's farsighted plans. For the students, it was an education in early childhood development. For the nursing home patients, it was a bridge with life in its earliest stages. For the infants, it was a cocoon of love and affection.

Because of Miri Mills's concepts for treating the aged with grace and dignity, Cali's elderly population prospered. They lived longer and more productive lives, suffering far fewer of the diseases associated with old age in other countries. Senile dementia was practically unknown and physical incapacities were quickly diagnosed and treated. The aged did not permit their infirmities to keep them in bed inasmuch as going to the theater or nursery was an activity not to be missed. These concepts resulted in an average Cali life span of more than one hundred years, despite that each individual was born in the United States, where the longevity was less than ninety. So the success of an effort to increase the quality and length of human life by bolstering the human spirit was an incontrovertible fact. A fact owed to the dreams and plans of a woman designated for exile by her native country.

Sadly, Miri did not live to enjoy the surroundings she had so methodically designed for her countrymen and countrywomen. At the age of seventy-seven, after again refusing to accept her party's nomination for prime minister, she suffered a premature heart attack while on a routine inspection of a nursing home in southern Cali. Cara, then deputy director of the Office for the Aging and Miri's assistant, was with her when it happened.

The early death of this wonderful woman who had done so much to advance and promote better living conditions for the aged cast a pall upon the entire country. Declaring it a national day of mourning, Miri's adopted homeland said good-bye with its first-ever state funeral. As Cara marched with the head of the procession, she had great difficulty maintaining her decorum.

As the plane continued smoothly on its course, Cara flipped back and forth through the briefing book reviewing the statistics related to Cali's nursing homes and longevity. The material was not new to her, but she wanted to be sure that she could quote from it without hesitation. Although Miri had been dead for several years, Cara considered the invitation to the conference to be a testimonial to the diminutive woman's devotion, and she wanted the world to know more about the accomplishments of one of the persons America had exiled.

Scanning the biographical data about Miri, Cara was deeply absorbed and didn't hear the copilot's knock on the door of the VIP lounge. "You almost scared the life out of me," she yelped as she looked up to see the boyish face smiling at her.

"Sorry, Ms. Romero. I just wanted to let you know that our landing destination has been changed to the Rockland Airport, just a few miles north of New York City. We should be landing in about twelve minutes."

Rushing in behind the departing copilot, Tim motioned to the windows. "The cloud cover is dissipating and you can actually see New York and Kennedy Airport. It's unbelievable," he said in an incredulous tone as Cara moved to the window. "Thousands of people are jamming the runway."

Peering between the clouds, she could see little specks moving back and forth like ants seeking sugar. As Tim had said, they numbered in the thousands, and although the plane in which they were flying required only one hundred feet for a safe landing, there didn't appear to be one hundred feet of unoccupied space within viewing distance.

"I just got a call from Michael Angelico, the liaison officer for the conference." He continued to stare out the window, shaking his head in amazement. "Angelico said that media personnel are ignoring the outcome of the lottery. Instead of twelve members of the press greeting you, every member of the press corps who ever wore an ID badge is out there. He advised us to land at Rockland instead. Angelico won't be able to get there in time to meet us, so we'll cab it to the hotel. Better get your running shoes on."

"Damn, I'm being deprived of my grand entrance." Cara put her papers back into the attaché case and began gathering her luggage for the debarkation.

"We've already been cleared by customs," said the copilot as they exited from the VIP lounge, "and we'll be landing in less than two minutes. We'll get as close to the Rockland terminal building as we possibly can. Then, you're on your own." He paused before reentering the cabin. "Good luck at the conference, Ms. Romero."

As soon as the plane touched the ground, they raced down the stairs with all their luggage in hand and dashed for the main terminus. Trying to appear casual, they entered the building and hand in hand blended with a crowd of incoming passengers from an adjoining airplane. They had not yet walked the length of the terminal to the street exit doors when they heard the announcement come over the loud speakers, "Paging Cara Romero. Paging Cara Romero." Cara's surprised reaction elicited a response from the woman who was walking next to her, "I can't believe it. I can't believe it. They must have landed at Rockland!" she yelped with delight. "I guess so," mumbled Cara as she held Tim closer.

Huddling together, heads practically touching in pretense of romantic ardor, they rushed out the door and pushed their way into a waiting cab, throwing their luggage into the topside storage bin with an unfamiliar ease.

The thirty-minute trip to the Southwind Hotel was made in almost complete silence except for an occasional affectionate murmur or theatrical kiss. Although Tim was almost sure that the driver could not hear any conversation, he did not want to take the chance of him being able to identify them and their destination. Once the change in landing sites became known, he was sure every cabbie in the Rockland area would be checking his trip ticket.

"I'm sure we look more like honeymooners than homosexuals from Cali," he whispered to Cara as he nuzzled her neck.

"I didn't know this was part of the assignment," she whispered back.

Casually entering the hotel, Tim strode up to the registration desk and announced the arrival of Mr. and Mrs. Andrew Smiley, the names in which their reservations were being held, to the waiting clerk. Cara lingered behind—just as they had rehearsed with Gary Kane—and waited for her husband to complete the forms and return with the key.

Giggling in nervous relief, they boarded the empty elevator and pushed the button for the thirty-fourth floor. Cara pressed her watch for a blood pressure check as she slumped against the wall.

Ten

They unlocked the door to 3408 to the sound of an insistent telephone. "I don't know that I'm ready for this. Maybe we should just ignore the ring," Cara said, collapsing into an overstuffed chair.

"Well, it's good to know that you're not bored by the life of a diplomat," said Tim as he reached for the phone switch. Turning it to one-way visual, he and Cara watched the pompous face of Michael Angelico fill the screen.

Michael Angelico looked like the maître d' of a bad French restaurant. Gray receding hair emphasized a forehead too broad for the rest of his face, a nose in the shape of a question mark, lips in a perpetual pucker, and ears that looked like they were ready to detach and return to the head to which they really belonged.

"Welcome to the Southwind, Mr. and Mrs. Smiley," he said with a sober expression. "With your permission, I'll be right up to meet with you."

Two minutes later, before they had a chance to recover from their thirty-fourth floor view of the concrete city, Angelico arrived.

"Mrs. Smiley," he began, "and I must call you that, because I don't dare use your real name—"

Cara quickly interrupted. "In fairness to the country I represent, Mr. Angelico, when you speak to me or about me, you should use the proper title of Ms., which in Cali indicates an uncommitted, or in your language, unmarried, woman. Nor is it necessary for you to call me by a name other than my own in the privacy of my room. I will not allow the American media to force me to change my name in my private living quarters."

Pleased by the firmness with which she had handled Angelico, Tim nodded encouragement.

doi:10.1300/5559_11

Angelico noticeably stiffened. "Of course." After a seemingly endless amount of throat clearing, he continued. "Ms. Romero, in view of the great interest the people of this country have in you and Cali, as demonstrated by the airport disturbance, for which I, incidentally, apologize, the conference committee has asked that you hold a press briefing prior to our first meeting. We are hopeful that the briefing will satisfy this nation's interest in you, personally, and enable us to get on with the business at hand."

Conducting this meeting in the formal manner she intended, Cara deferred to Tim, who, as escort officer, served as both her bodyguard and her public relations representative.

"Before we proceed with a press briefing, Mr. Angelico, we need your full assurances that the briefings will be conducted under the highest security for Ms. Romero. We will want a full credentials and weapons check as well as security personnel on all entrances to the building and the meeting room during the briefing, and during the conference's subsequent meeting. If you are in agreement with those conditions, I see no reason why we cannot acquiesce to your request."

"Mr. Felmar, do you really think all that security is necessary? After all, we are a civilized society and we respect Ms. Romero as being the representative of a world government. I do not believe——"

Tim did not allow Angelico to finish his sentence. "Civilized, but violent," he interjected. "New York has more murders in one day than Cali does in one year. My country would not be happy with me if I did not take the proper steps to ensure the protection of our representatives. I will call you in the morning to make sure that all such matters receive proper attention."

To be sure that Angelico had no doubts about Tim's authority, Cara joined the conversation. "He speaks for Cali," she stated with finality.

After discussing some additional details of the security requirements and the press briefing, Angelico left, but not before asking a question that they were to hear many times on this New York visit.

"Ms. Romero," he began almost humbly, "I promised my sister that I would ask for your personal assistance on a matter of great importance to my family." He hesitated.

"Yes, please continue."

"Twelve years ago, my younger sister, Leona, sent her firstborn child to Cali. He was a much loved three-year-old child. Of course, we have heard nothing since. Leona has never been the same. She begged me to ask you if there is any way you can find out how Alberto is doing. Is he still alive? Is he happy?"

Cara noted the discomfort with which he asked the questions and wondered whether his body language was the result of his sorrow over the loss of Alberto or embarrassment at having to ask a lesbian for help.

"I am sorry, Mr. Angelico, but there is absolutely nothing I can do to help you or your sister. Documents relating to the birth identity of Cali's citizens are very carefully guarded, rated top secret by your country and priority-one by mine. The only information given to the Calian adoptive parent or parents concerns essential health and medical data. I am sorry. I can do nothing for you."

Resuming his diplomatic role as though the personal request had never been made, Angelico bowed slightly. "Thank you for meeting with me, Ms. Romero. I will be present at tomorrow's briefing and look forward to seeing you then." He turned to Tim, practically clicking his heels before he spoke. "I will call you in the morning to confirm the briefing plans. I am sure you will be very well satisfied with our security arrangements."

Angelico was barely out the door when Tim and Cara ran to their luggage and began changing into evening wear for their first night in America.

"These clothes have no style at all," he groaned.

Tim was right, of course. Even though they had carefully chosen the best clothes available at the simulated American store, they still looked drab. Because of prohibitions against exporting, Cali's futuristic clothes and vibrant transparent materials were not yet being shared with the rest of the world. That would all change one day, Cara supposed. Her generation did not share the elders' isolationist policies and they certainly did not object to inflating Cali's treasury with heterosexual money.

"After the airport experience, I'm actually glad we have these American clothes. It makes it much easier for us to blend. Besides, there's no one to impress. The only people who will notice us on the streets of New York will be those of the wrong sex."

"Let's hit those streets," yelled Tim, and they both bolted for the door, laughing like two children who had just tasted the shared joy of a secret.

Eleven

Of the five senses, smell was undoubtedly Cara's worst. Although she could distinguish the odor of pungent garlic from that of sweet Sappho Perfume, the aromas between evaded her. So, it surprised her almost as much as it did Tim when she reacted so quickly to the New York air that assailed her nostrils as they exited through the hotel's revolving door.

"What is that smell?" she asked, crinkling her nose in horror.

"That, my dear Cara, is the sweet aroma of garbage which spills out from those containers," he pointed to metal cans lining the sidewalk, "into the city's streets. New York never installed an underground refuse collection system. There was an old subway and it could have been converted for garbage control, but the tunnels had become homes for the city's poor. The authorities do not want to force the poor to return aboveground, so the availability of underground facilities has been ignored. Only when a body needs to be removed or raw sewage pumped out do officials even acknowledge that the subway tunnels exist. Internationally, New York is known as 'Shitty City.'"

"No wonder this city has such critical health problems. The air alone is enough to make one sick. I must have been too busy running from reporters to notice it before. Now, it's overwhelming."

They continued their walk without conversation, Cara engrossed in the city's landscape. Everything was so different from Cali. The streets and buildings were of a dull gray cement. The colorful plastics that dominated her country were not in evidence, nor were the outdoor gardens or saplings or the architectural accents of glass and contrasting synthetics. Stores were everywhere—row after row of all kinds of stores: food, clothing, pet, liquor, and religious. Lots of religious. Litter, too, was everywhere. The streets were dotted with garbage of var-

doi:10.1300/5559_12

ious colors and sizes. Pedestrians stepped over it, next to it, and into it. Those pedestrians, of course, looked just like Calians, with one notable exception—men did not hold hands with men, nor did women with women. As visibly demonstrated, Americans were attracted to members of the opposite sex.

As they approached the third intersection of their walk Cara became aware of the numbers of women standing on each corner. She and Tim stopped, pretended to be looking into a store window, and silently watched as one sashayed over to a car stopped for a red light. She was a big woman, with long stringy yellow hair piled high atop her head, dressed in all green: green scoop neck blouse, green short skirt, green stockings, and green boots. As she pivoted her body to speak to the driver, her skirt flared, flashing a hint of green tights. The light changed and the driver pressed hard on the gas pedal. Jumping back, the woman looked at them and smiled. *The woman knows we are looking at her,* thought Cara, and to her surprise, she found the interaction almost sensual.

"I really shouldn't be staring," she motioned to Tim to move on, "but I've never seen a woman prostitute before. I'm used to seeing an occasional male, but not a female."

"It's a good thing," he said, acknowledging her blushing cheeks.

"And it's so ironic," she continued. "They all seem to be standing in front of churches. But, I guess that's usual when you consider that almost every other building is devoted to religion. Why?"

"That's an easy one to answer. After gays left the country and Olmstead became president, the religionists confiscated the companies and homes that had been relinquished by the émigrés. They seized the property in the name of the church and then erected assembly halls and church-related businesses. Eventually, of course, the citizens objected to supporting all these houses of worship, particularly because the dwellers in the houses were repeatedly involved in scandals of major financial proportions. So now, most of the churches are merely facades, housing nothing but empty halls." He paused. "Of course, the fact that America has all these churches contributes to the country's hunger problems. Churches and church-related businesses do not pay taxes and that makes this country very poor."

Entering the restaurant that Tim had picked, Cara visibly applauded. With deliberate selectivity, he had chosen the Mayflower, a restaurant built before the 2020 World Environmental Acts prohibited the use of wood in commercial eating establishments. The elegant surroundings were in sharp contrast to places like Topanga's, where Cara frequently dined. In Cali, even the most formal of restaurants were devoid of wood, fashioned mainly in plastic and glass with emphasis on natural decorations of plants and flowers. Aquariums, once the rage, were no longer being used because of the increasing number of endangered fish. In the newer eateries, upscale fashion was double glass walls in which beads of many colors were placed for a nice light effect, but one that was becoming common and failed to encourage intimate evenings. But the Mayflower, with beige marble entry floors and black granite edging, and massive beveled mirrors that danced light into crystal chandeliers, surrounded one with intimacy. Cara stroked the burnished mahogany railing that led into the main dining area and wished she was with a woman.

After being seated, they began watching the other diners, trying to be as casual as curiosity could allow. And they were curious. Most of the tables were occupied by parties of two, a man and woman—a strange sight to Cara and Tim. They stared in fascination, Cara commenting softly on the actions and gestures that were so similar to those she exchanged with her female lovers—a touch of hands, coy smiles, an occasional wink. Seeing such interaction between members of opposite sexes seemed perverse. They observed differences too. The women appeared to defer to the men and the men appeared more solicitous of the women. Men remained standing until the women took their seats; men ordered the meals; men tasted the wine. They could not stop watching.

"My innate nature must be that of a voyeur," said Tim.

Other sights were strange to the eyes of the Calians. The sexes were intermingled at tables where there were children. Male and female parents sat together with their biological offspring who were of both sexes. In Cali, where there was no such thing as a biological child, committed females raised female children and committed males raised male children. So, one rarely saw tables of intermingled sexes, unless opposite-sex friends got together with their respective children for a group meal.

"We are so different and yet so similar to our American counterparts," she observed.

"Would you like to order?" Tim smiled at the beautiful woman who was suddenly younger than her thirty-two years, almost a child again in this foreign atmosphere.

The food disappointed them. Ordering chicken in a marsala wine sauce, Cara had anticipated a taste with which she was familiar, but the flavor evaded her experiences. The broiled steak Tim described as "horrible . . . more like pork."

"It must be our scientific farming and pollution-free environment that makes the difference," he volunteered. "We grow the best produce, vegetables, and herbs. Our chickens are raised naturally with the best feed. We have modern cattle farms and fish farms. Our menu ingredients are the best. How can our food not be superior?"

Relaxing after the heavy meal, they sat sipping an herbal tea and reviewing the press briefing for the next day when Cara noticed a young attractive woman at the opposite table. She sat with an older lady, her mother perhaps. To her surprise, the two women actually looked alike. Even more surprising, they dressed alike, both wearing bright floral print blouses with the awkwardly puffed sleeves that seemed so common in American fashion. Never having seen parents and children from the same biological family before that day, she was truly fascinated and continued to stare. The physical similarities astonished her. Both were small boned with brown eyes, light brown hair, perky noses, and small ears. In silhouette, their faces were versions of each other. As she continued to look at the younger woman, their eyes met and the woman smiled in her direction several times. A few minutes later, Cara noticed that she was still looking their way, coyly lowering her eyes to the carpeted floor when Cara caught her glance.

"Tim, I can't really believe it, but I think I'm being cruised."

"Don't believe it. It's me she's interested in. She's been flirting with me since we sat down."

"Oh, I am embarrassed. I just never saw a woman look at a man as a sex object. That's so strange to these lesbian eyes."

They laughed, and as they did, she saw Tim in a way that she had not seen him before. He was handsome. At six foot three he had the beautiful muscular body of the trained gymnast and the chiseled features that hinted of a Greek heritage. His black hair was darker than the black eyes that sparkled with each smile, a perfect contrast to his lover Glen whom he teasingly referred to as "my golden boy." Cara wondered about her appearance with Tim. Did the young woman think they were a couple or did she assume they were brother and sister? They had very different coloring. Did it matter? Such thoughts were new to her.

"Don't you think most of the media questions will be about you and your life in Cali?" he was asking.

Trying to concentrate on the conversation, she faced him squarely, putting her hands to her face like blinders on a horse. "This is the first time that a Calian has ever granted an interview to the American press. Because of the failure of America's history books to deal honestly with this country's role in the establishment of Cali, I'm sure specific questions will be asked. I want you to know that I have been authorized by the governing council to answer truthfully."

"No problem. That's the way it should be," replied Tim, smiling in response to the floral bloused woman who walked deliberately close to their table on her way to the restroom.

"Tim," she asked, "why do you think they hate us?"

"Because we're different from them. Because they don't know how to act in our presence. Because they feel foolish, maybe even rejected, when we don't respond to their flirtations."

"I read a theory once suggesting that heterosexual men have the biggest problem with homosexuals because they fear having other men treat them as though they are women, the sex they consider inferior. That says a lot about the way straight men perceive women." She watched as the woman returned to her table, smiling again at Tim. For the slightest moment, she felt offended at being ignored.

When they finished their tea, they took a taxi back to the hotel. "New York is not safe at night," said Tim.

Twelve

⤙∾♆∾⤚

Mornings were Cara's best time. Each one began a new twenty-four-hour adventure to be enjoyed, savored, and relished. Tim disagreed. "Tomorrow, go to breakfast without me if it's before nine a.m.," he mumbled before falling asleep almost immediately upon their return to the Southwind.

It was 6:00 a.m. when she awoke, the equivalent of 3:00 a.m. Cali time, but she could not return to sleep, her thoughts kept alert by visions of the prostitutes and the restaurant. Taking a quick shower, she dressed in American clothes, left a note for Tim, and descended to the lobby in time for the opening of the coffee shop.

Although the lobby appeared crowded for the early hour, she noticed nothing strange and devoured her eggs and potatoes with customary zeal. It was only when the waitress brought coffee that she became aware of unusual activities.

"Isn't it exciting?" she asked as she placed the cup before Cara. "They think the Calian homosexuals are staying at the Southwind."

"That sure is exciting," she said, beads of perspiration instantly forming along the base of her neck.

"Yeah, I'm so flustered by it all, I just keep dropping things and banging into customers," the waitress jabbered, arms flapping as she spoke. "And one of the newspaper reporters just told me that they were able to get in secretly by dressing as two guys. I don't know how they managed that." Lowering her head as is if betraying a confidence, she whispered, "I heard the woman is really quite a looker. Beautiful, they say."

The orange juice was squirming in her stomach, but the temptation to pursue the conversation was greater than her budding nausea. "Really! What does she look like?"

doi:10.1300/5559_13

"Black hair, cut very short and mannish, blue eyes, tall and slim, they say. Speaks tough. Almost like a man. I'm keeping my eyes peeled in case she comes in on my shift. It'll be a thousand dollars if I find her for that reporter." She nodded toward a tall lanky man who was draped over a woman sitting at the counter.

"I'll keep my eyes open for you." *Forgive me my lies,* she thought silently.

"Hey, thanks. Really, that's very nice of you." She refilled the cup, smiled wordlessly, and moved on to the next table.

Cara finished her coffee slowly, chewing feebly on a piece of wheat toast, trying not to appear in too much of a hurry, and watched as the crowd grew in the lobby. It began to loom large. Media personnel, she was sure.

Looking out the window of the Southwind coffee shop, she saw a small group of six or seven men and women gathering at the corner opposite the hotel. Their leader, the shortest among them, a slightly overweight middle-aged man with a ruddy complexion, stood in the middle shouting instructions. A pickup truck pulled to the curb and he ran over, vigorously hauling down signs and distributing them to the others, pointing energetically to the Southwind. Cara watched as the band of Olms spread out in front of the Bonner Street entrance to the coffee shop, demanding attention from anyone passing by with a camera. "Fags Burn in Hell," read one sign. "Lesbians Are Sick," said another.

"Those shmucks are at it again," shrugged one man as he hid his camera in his jacket pocket before exiting the restaurant.

When enough time had passed to allay suspicion, Cara nonchalantly walked to the register, gave the pasty-faced cashier the check signed "Mrs. Andrew Smiley, room 3408," and made her way through the milling groups of reporters to the elevator.

Tim was still groggy when she flung open the door to the room, but was fully alert by the time she had closed it and sat down on the bed. She began relating the events of the morning when Tim suddenly grabbed her and pulled her down on top of him, kissing her somewhere in the region of the ear as he did so. Before she had a chance to react, she heard the feminine voice coming from behind her.

"Sorry. Sorry. My mistake. I thought this room was empty," said the woman in a maid's uniform whose body was framed by the doorway, the keys still jingling in her hand.

Tim released her as the door closed. He gently cupped his hand over her mouth and put a finger to his lips as they listened quietly to the same voice apologizing in the next room.

"It looks like she was also offered a thousand dollars. Or maybe she's an enterprising reporter," said Tim. "Well, I guess I'd better call Angelico and see if different arrangements can be made for us or if they want us to stay here and ride this out." He playfully tugged on her long blonde hair. "Short black hair, indeed. They did get the eye color right, but there ain't nothing mannish about you. Wish there was."

"Who knows? If you keep kissing me, I may be forced to change my orientation."

They decided that she should call Angelico while Tim showered and prepared for the press briefing. He answered immediately. "Angelico speaking."

After she explained, in as few words as possible, their predicament and the presence of picketers from the Olms, there was a long pause and a series of beeps. *Oh great,* she thought, *we've been cut off.*

"I was checking to make sure the line was secure," he explained as he came back on. "It is. Now, please listen to me carefully. Pack your bags and be ready to move. You will not be going back to the Southwind after today's session. This afternoon, I will have my security personnel pick up your luggage and transfer it to your new location. Leave your things on the bed, put a 'do not disturb' sign on the hall doorknob, and tell the hotel desk clerk that you are going out for a short while and do not wish maid service. Take a cab to the conference site security entrance. I will wait for you there. I'm going to repeat these instructions for you once more." And he did, almost verbatim. "Do you understand, Ms. Romero?"

"Mr. Angelico, I'm a lesbian, not an idiot," she snarled as she turned off the phone switch.

"What was that all about?" asked Tim as he walked into the room, a towel wrapped around his waist.

"That man is irritating the shit out of me," she said as she related the conversation.

"He may be a jerk, but it sounds like he knows his stuff. Clear, concise, and to the point. Can't ask for more." He paused thoughtfully and added with a smile, "Well, I guess we could ask for a gay person, but I really don't think there are any on the American diplomats' list."

"That's the trouble with this country," she grumbled as she began emptying the drawers she had filled the night before.

They complied with Angelico's instructions, stopped at the coffee shop so that Tim could have breakfast, and were ready to leave before noon. The last thing that Cara did before departing the hotel was look up the name Barbra Weissman in the lobby's New York area computer. There was no such listing.

Thirteen

As they exited through the Southwind's revolving door, a small group of reporters rushed up to them. "Nah, it can't be her," muttered one of the men despairingly. "She's beautiful."

"Who says a lesbian can't be beautiful?" asked the lone female in the group. "I'm sure there are beautiful lesbians . . . just like there are ugly men," she yelled after them as they walked away.

Cara let go of Tim's hand and turned to look at the plump woman with chipmunk cheeks who challengingly stared back. "It's okay," said Cara, "I agree with you. I'm sure there are beautiful lesbians. And ugly men."

The woman started to giggle and as she saw Cara start to grin, she laughed more heartily, until the two of them were doubled over with laughter. "These men just make me so angry. Opinionated people don't belong in the press corps. Matter of fact, they don't belong anywhere." She extended her hand and shook Cara's vigorously, "My name is Sherry Ryan. Thank you for that wonderful moment. You've a great laugh." She didn't wait for a response, but began walking toward the hotel door.

Cara walked toward Tim, changed her mind, and ran back after the woman, grabbing her arm. "Look, I just heard that the Calians are going to hold a press briefing at the World Conference Center at two p.m. Maybe that's where you ought to be."

"Thanks. That means I won't have to stay here much longer, but there's no sense in me going to the conference center today—I wouldn't be allowed into their press briefing. I don't have the credentials. I'm a junior reporter and a woman. And not even a beautiful woman." A mischievous grin spread across her face, casting glitter into the pale brown eyes.

doi:10.1300/5559_14

Without hesitation, Cara reached into her shoulder bag and pulled out a business card. Turning it over, she wrote on the back, "Admit Sherry Ryan, Unopinionated Woman Reporter with a Beautiful Smile." She handed it to her and jumped into the waiting cab before the junior reporter had a chance to react.

"What was that all about?" asked Tim as they passed the Olms, their numbers down to blue cap and two others.

"I never expected to find a lesbian-friendly reporter in New York City. I thought she deserved a reward."

"Are you sure there wasn't more to it than that?"

"Absolutely sure. But maybe we've made a media friend, and that's something we can always use."

As the cab approached 42nd Street and First Avenue, Tim instructed the driver to use the security entrance. He did so without hesitation and then jubilantly asked for their autographs. "Just wait till Mary sees this. Just you wait," he mumbled to himself in broken English.

"Even the cab drivers know about us." She sighed.

———— ⁓❦⁓ ————

Michael Angelico, standing inside the VIP lobby of the conference center, was not surprised to feel the bulge in the front of his pants when he saw them entering through the security doors. *She is stunning,* he thought silently. *Absolutely gorgeous.* He wondered if she had ever been with a man.

"Forget it," whispered Tim, glaring down at the diplomat's crotch.

"Did I miss something?" asked Cara.

"I hope so." He took her elbow and guided her past the startled man whose erection shrank in dismay. Catching up from behind, a red-faced Angelico escorted them to a third-floor conference room adjoining the auditorium in which the press briefing was going to be held.

"Please make yourselves comfortable. We have complied with all of your requests, and the only people on the premises right now are security personnel. The press will not be allowed in the building until one-thirty. There's a carafe of coffee on the table. Now, is there anything else I can do for you?"

"You can tell us where we will be living for the next three weeks," said Cara as she admiringly ran her hand across the surface of the brightly polished solid oak table. "This is beautiful."

"Thank you." He hesitated. "Quite frankly, Mrs. Smi—excuse me, Ms. Romero—that decision has not yet been made. I have made several phone calls to my superiors and I am sure I will have the answer to your question before the end of today's session. However, let me assure you, your luggage is being picked up by our security personnel right now." He stopped to scratch an imaginary itch on the back of his neck. "Your belongings will be properly secured."

"We're not worried about our belongings," said Tim. "It's our bodies we're worried about."

"Please do not concern yourselves. I am sure my superiors will take the essential steps to protect you."

"Just keep in mind that the Olms know we're here."

"Mr. Felmar, the whole world knows you're here." He smiled woodenly. "But you needn't worry about the Olms. This building is fully secured. You will be quite safe. In the interim, if you need me, press the buzzer on the wall by the door." He bowed slightly and exited the room after a seemingly endless session of throat clearing.

As soon as he left, Tim got up and looked around, making sure that the door to the auditorium was locked and the telephone was working. "Well," he said, "this room seems safe enough. I guess I'd better start earning my money and go through the rest of the building. Now, I'm going to leave you here by yourself, but you'll be fine. Nobody knows who you are yet, so you don't have to bother locking the entrance door. If anybody comes in, just tell them you're Mrs. Smiley or something." He grinned, clicked his heels, bowed slightly, and was gone.

Pleased to be left alone, Cara walked around the room touching everything. A wooden table, wooden chairs, parquet floors. Even storage cabinets made of wood. She ran her hand across each and thought about how it felt. To her surprise, each kind of wood had a different texture. Some rough, some bumpy, but mostly smooth. The highly polished table felt cold to her hand. Like glass, she thought, or a mirror. Or even the plastic of Cali. Bending down, she sniffed at the tabletop but was disappointed when she could detect no discernible odor. She got down on the floor on her hands and knees and tried smelling the parquet. Then she heard the doorknob turning.

"May I help you? Are you okay?" asked a woman's voice, rushing toward her. "Did you fall? Did you hurt yourself?" She reached under the table and put her hand on Cara's shoulder.

Too stunned to move at first, Cara suddenly jumped to her feet, almost knocking over the good Samaritan who stepped aside and quickly began walking backward toward the door. "I'm sorry. I didn't mean to. . . . I'm sorry. I thought the room was empty."

"No. No. It's okay," said a startled Cara, brushing herself off as she self-consciously stared at the face of the most sensuous woman she had ever seen. *American Indian,* she thought. *She's got to be American Indian. Or Greek. Maybe Greek.* Copper skin of porcelain with black cherubic ringlets framing a face just wide enough to accommodate the oversized muted gray eyes. Her prominent cheekbones narrowed down to a strong chin separated in the middle by a seductive cleft. If there was a flaw, and Cara wasn't sure there was, it was the perky nose that compromised the expression in her sober eyes. She moved deftly as she opened the door, obviously comfortable in her lithe body. A miniature of Cara's own, it was more delicate and petite but flowed with the same graceful, fluid lines.

"I'm early for the briefing and I thought I could wait in here. But I'll wait in the hall." She raised an amused eyebrow, the left corner of her lips turning up ever so slightly, as she watched Cara scramble for composure.

She exited quickly, too quickly for Cara to do anything except mumble "Okay," more to herself than to the young reporter.

She sat down and ran her hand through the hair that fell carelessly on her forehead. I'm glad Tim isn't around to ask me how I feel about this woman, she sighed.

Taking some paper from her attaché case, she spent the rest of the time preparing an opening statement. Although the briefing would primarily be a question-and-answer session, there were some sentiments she wanted to express at the beginning in response to the silent questions of those who, like Angelico's sister, were still grieving their lost children. She was making her final notes when the door opened. Her disappointment was palpable when she saw that it was Tim.

"Anything happen while I was gone?"

"No," she said. "Not a thing."

Fourteen

The press briefing began promptly at 2:00 p.m. in an auditorium filled to capacity. The reporters, chattering in hushed tones as they exchanged information about the Calians, quickly silenced when Angelico introduced "Cara Romero, Cali's Director of the Office for the Aging and our guest at the World Conference."

As she confidently walked onto the stage, she heard an audible gasp from the audience. She was used to that. Even in her own country where attractive women were commonplace, people reacted with surprise when she was introduced in her official capacity. But never did she enjoy the reaction more than now.

Tim, standing in the back of the room observing the security procedures, looked up in open-mouthed admiration. In the fifteen minutes he had left her alone to prepare for her entrance, she had changed to a full Calian body suit, carefully concealed in the security compartment of her attaché case.

Comprised of three layers of progressively lighter diaphanous material, the single-piece lavender outfit was cut into a modest V-neck with a slimming waistline held together by the palest yellow floor-length sash. The bell-cut legs flowed, barely skirting the parquet as she moved across the stage. Single-layered tight sleeves of a scarcely visible lemon shade molded to her well-defined arms, emphasizing the graceful movements of an athlete. Her soft blonde hair added height to the continuum of style and color. The combination of woman and clothes was magnificent.

Taking her position at the podium, she waited for her eyes to adjust to the lights and peered down at the assemblage. Scanning quickly, she spotted the beautiful young Samaritan in the last row. Her breath caught as her eyes focused on the incredibly sculptured face.

doi:10.1300/5559_15

Patiently, she waited for the audience to quiet down, winked at Sherry Ryan, who sat smiling in the front row, calmly put her notes on the lectern, and began speaking in the loud, clear voice of the politician.

"Ladies and gentlemen of the press, it is with great pride that I come here today to speak before you. Pride as a lesbian. Pride as a Calian . . . and pride as an American . . . because I am that too. I was born in this country in the year 2023, the child of anonymous parents. Anonymous not by choice but by legislation—legislation caused by the religionists in this country who, upon postulating that homosexuality was evil, created an environment that mandated my banishment. And so this three-year-old, in the company of 4,000 other youngsters who had tested positive for the Scarpetti gene, was put on a ship and made a ward of the country of Cali." She paused for emphasis. "And now, ladies and gentlemen, I want to thank you for that voyage. Twenty-nine years ago, you sent me to a budding country, replete with the love and enthusiasm born from adversity. And twenty-nine years later, I can say that I am from one of the finest, most progressive nations on earth—a nation in which crime is practically unknown, health care is universal, and the elderly live in the dignity earned by their years. I am proud of who I am and I am proud of where I'm from. To all Americans, I bring this message from the people of my country: Do not grieve for your anonymous children. Take joy, instead, in their liberation and in the fullness of their lives as Calians. Their voyage is sweet, their destination, even sweeter."

She stopped speaking and waited for the audience's reaction. When none was forthcoming, she stated, "Thank you for giving me the opportunity to speak. I will now entertain your questions."

Slowly, almost casually, the applause began. Rhythmic at first, it soon lost all sense of balance and threatened to vibrate the walls. People standing at the sides began stomping and soon the whole audience was standing and stomping. Cara, embarrassed by the response, held her hands up signaling them to stop. Gradually order was restored.

The question-and-answer period began. The reporters were brief and to the point. No embarrassing questions were asked until the session was almost at an end.

"Have you ever been with a male?" asked a muscular young man who stood in the back of the room.

"Have you?" she responded quickly, eliciting laughter from the audience.

The raven-haired Samaritan in the back row stood up. "I apologize for the rudeness of my countryman. He works for a newspaper that we hold in very low esteem." Without another word, she turned, deftly moved to the aisle, and left the auditorium, exiting the door next to which Tim was standing.

Cara terminated the briefing. "That will be all for today. Thank you for your attendance. If you wish to schedule a personal interview, please see Michael Angelico, the liaison for the Conference. I will try to accommodate as many requests as possible. Thank you again." She quickly gathered her papers and rushed out the stage exit.

The Samaritan was standing near the elevator. Hesitantly, Cara began walking toward her and then stopped. *What would I say,* she thought. *What could I possibly say?*

"You were wonderful," said Sherry Ryan, approaching from behind.

"Thank you." Cara turned her back to the elevator and faced the pudgy woman.

"You've given us a new perspective on Cali. You're going to get really good press out of this. Especially from me. I want to thank you for getting me into the briefing. I appreciate it. Maybe I can take you to lunch sometime. Or dinner. Or how 'bout a drink?"

"Oh, that really isn't necessary. Thanks for the offer, but the next three weeks are going to be quite hectic."

"I know it's not necessary, but it's something I would like to do. I'll ask you about it again as soon as the conference begins," she said smilingly as she backed away, turning to leave.

"Whoops," said Tim as Sherry bumped into him. After a profusion of apologies, she continued walking down the hall. He turned mischievously to Cara. "Are you sure—"

"I'm sure," she interrupted.

"Look, don't let this go to your head, but that was one hell of a speech. And I'll tell you, you really had some of those guys going with your appearance. I don't think there was a dry crotch in the room except for mine."

"Tim!"

"Sorry. Couldn't resist," he declared with a naughty-boy grin. "Okay, it's almost three p.m. now and you have some people waiting for you in the auditorium. Press boys, I think. While you're attending to them, I'm going to find Angelico and get some definite info on our living arrangements. I do think you should consider changing your clothes before we go into the outer world, however. That does not exactly blend with the American style."

She winked as she left to return to the auditorium.

Tim watched her walk down the hall and wondered if she realized just how much respect she had garnered for Cali during that briefing. It was more than her appearance. It was her demeanor, her bearing, the manner in which she spoke, the confident way she carried herself. There was a grace to the woman, a presence that transcended sexuality.

After seeing her enter the auditorium, he began his own hunt, looking for Michael Angelico. When he finally located the press office, Tim was not surprised to find Angelico on the phone. *This is a man who does better on the phone than in person,* he thought.

"I think we've solved the problem in the very best way possible, Mr. Felmar," he began as he turned off the receiver. "You and Ms. Romero, as guests of this country, will be staying at the president's New York retreat for the duration of your visit. It's located on Long Island, near the community of Stony Brook, only minutes from this building by helicopter."

"Is it secure?"

"Oh yes, very. The estate was originally owned by Ellyn Hargreaves, the famous blues singer, who, I believe, is now a resident of Cali. She . . . uh, uh . . . donated the house to the government before she departed the country. It is a perfect presidential retreat. Because of Ellyn Hargreaves's celebrity status, she had installed burglar alarms and special security devices. Additionally, you will have the protection of secret service personnel who are on the premises at all times to protect it from sabotage and vandalism. They are there even when the president is in DC. Yes. It's very safe."

"How about transportation arrangements?"

"I was just taking care of that when you entered. You will be traveling by presidential limousine. Your driver will be Leonard Malta, a senior member of the security forces. In the event of an emergency, helicopter transportation will be made available. We have taken every step necessary for your safety and comfort."

"You know, Angelico, I'm becoming more and more impressed with your efficiency. I'm sure you've made some kind of preparation for food."

An unsmiling but obviously pleased Angelico responded, "But, of course. The president's personal housekeeper-cook is on the premises. She will take care of all meals."

"Thank you," said Tim. "Thank you very much."

Fifteen

―⁓⧉⧉⁓―

"So, how did your meeting with the press go?" asked Tim as they were settling into the limousine.

"They weren't from the press. They were international homosexual representatives to the conference who arrived early and decided to attend the briefing. The two men represent Sweden and there's an elderly lesbian named Liza from Denmark."

"Now, do I have to worry about your behavior with her?"

"If she were fifty years younger, you might. She's a charmer and very attractive, but Liza is eighty-five years old and not interested in twinkies."

They rode in silence for a while when Tim, turning to comment on the flatness of the surrounding countryside, discovered that Cara was fast asleep, her head resting comfortably on the attaché case that held her Calian clothes.

Startled awake by the sound of the security gates opening, Cara was surprised to discover that she had slept during the drive to Stony Brook. "But I never nap during the day," she protested.

"Well, you did on this day," he responded.

The estate, unfolding with each twist and turn of the pebbled roadway, was magnificent. Thickly wooded areas displayed the century-old gnarled trees that had disappeared from Cali's landscape during the fires that followed the 2018 earthquake. Warbling in harmony, caravans of birds flew hither and yon as the car emerged from the forest and entered into the flats of rolling blue-green lawns. After a few seconds, the massive house majestically appeared before them, a testament to the architecture predominant in the United States in the 1990s: wood, glass, and angular lines. It was a powerful building, befitting the woman they knew to be Ellyn Hargreaves.

doi:10.1300/5559_16

"Welcome. I'm Mrs. Anderson, the housekeeper of the Marion Estate," said the round-faced elderly woman as she opened the limousine door for them. Standing there with her bright green checkered dress and her starched white apron and cap, they had no doubt that the estate was cared for with meticulous efficiency.

"Michael Angelico said that this was the estate of Ellyn Hargreaves. Who's this Marion?" asked a surprised Tim, stretching his long legs after clambering out behind Cara.

"Well, it was named in 2024, after President Olmstead's wife. Name of Marion." She smiled proudly, pleased that she knew the answer.

"Some questions are better left unasked," muttered Cara under her breath.

Following behind Mrs. Anderson, who assured them that a secret service man would take care of their luggage, the Calians entered the building through massive wooden doors that led into a ballroom-size room. Straight ahead, through a semicircular wall of unobstructed glass, were the serene dark waters of the Long Island Sound, spawning an illusion that the cliffside house was eerily suspended over an abyss. Humming softly overhead, a motor drew back the thin cypress strips that covered a second level of window wall, exposing sky and puffed clouds beneath the eighteen-foot-high cedar-striped ceiling. Smells of wood and water wafted through the air.

"Ellyn always had good taste," mused Cara. Turning to Tim, she whispered, "That one you should have worried about."

"But . . . she's more than twenty years older than you."

"Sometimes age is not a factor."

"Eh? The age of this house?" interjected Mrs. Anderson. "It's about sixty years old. Did you have any other questions before we move on to your bedrooms?"

Upstairs, they were shown only their sleeping rooms. The other eight or nine doors were kept closed. Located on opposite sides of the hall, their luxurious suites were similar in size and appearance. Cara's view, however, was superior. From the small balcony accessed by French doors she could watch the waves of the sound slurping against the pristine beach several hundred feet below. She was reminded of

home and the deep blue of the Pacific, although the sound was noticeably quieter. Unlike the ocean, which was host to a continuous stream
of ships and pleasure boats, the sound appeared serene, almost for-
saken.

"Now, Mr. Felmar, Mr. Angelico told me to be sure to show you
the alarm systems and how they work, eh? So, if you'll come with me,
I'm sure Ms. Romero would like to be left alone to do her unpacking.
Dinner will be served promptly at eight," she said, looking at her, "in
the dining room that adjoins the main room."

After they left, Cara quickly explored the room. Larger than the
Southwind Hotel room, it contained a canopy bed, a desk, several
chairs, enough dresser drawers for a year-long visit, and a divan
placed romantically in front of the fireplace. Neat piles of woodless
ecological logs stood on the hearth. The French doors led to the balcony, and a gray door led to a bathroom. Inside, there was a toilet, a
bidet, two sinks, and a soul mates shower for two. "Fat chance of
that," she mumbled aloud.

After unpacking, she decided to find her way to the beach so she
could watch a midsummer sunset over the sound. Exiting from an
open door in the main room, she found herself on a grassy plateau
overlooking wooden steps that led down the side of the cliff. Eagerly,
she climbed down the stairs, surprised to see the edge of a swimming
pool off to the side of the next plateau.

Reaching the hexagon-shaped pool, she walked along the slate
deck, admiring the pink and gray marble structure that featured an
aqua jet at each of the six joints. Mists of tinted water sprayed into the
air, forming a pink fluid silk screen suspended between sky and water.
As she walked to the western end of the pool, she suddenly realized
she was not alone. Straight ahead, a woman sat facing the sunset. Approaching slowly, she tried not to scare her, but just as she drew
alongside the startled woman jumped up, almost falling when she
turned to face Cara.

"Good grief, you scared me," gasped the incredibly attractive
woman Cara had met in the conference room five hours earlier.

"What . . . What are you doing here?" asked Cara, embarrassed
that these were the only words she could think of to say.

"I live here," the Samaritan said hastily as she wrapped a towel around her nude body.

"You live here," Cara repeated, suddenly aware that she had been staring at the exquisite naked body of the most sensuous woman she had ever seen. "But . . . aren't you a reporter?"

"God forbid," she laughed. "I'm a marine biologist." Clumsily, trying to hold her towel with one hand, she put out the other to shake Cara's. "I'm Jessica Mooran, President Mooran's daughter. I guess we're destined to meet under awkward circumstances."

"Yes, it seems so. I . . . uh . . . just came down here to see the sunset. I didn't mean to intrude. But . . . let me make sure I understand this. You are the same woman I saw in the conference room today."

"You mean the one who found you on your hands and knees?" she asked with a glint in her eyes, her left eyebrow raised. "Yes. And I also attended the press briefing. Actually, I was in the building to get some data for the conference's opening on Wednesday. I'll be presenting the welcoming speech for my father."

Five days till Wednesday, thought Cara quickly. *Five wonderful days to enjoy this place and this woman.*

"Now, if you'll excuse me, I need to get upstairs and start getting ready for dinner. Will you and Mr. Felmar be joining me?"

"Yes. Is that all right?"

"I'd like that very much."

"Good," she smiled, feeling the redness of her heart as it pounded in her chest.

She watched Jessica's lean form disappear up the cliffside stairs, and then sat down in the chaise her body had vacated. Droplets of water puddled on the vinyl straps, evidence of its previous occupant. Absentmindedly, Cara pushed at the droplets, feeling the fluid warmth on her fingers. *I must be crazy,* she thought, as she felt her body responding to thoughts of Jessica. *This is a heterosexual, Scarpetti-gene negative woman. The president's daughter. Nothing can come of this.*

Forcing her mind to other things, she reflected on the events of her first full day in New York—an extraordinary series of activities. She had awakened in the Southwind Hotel in New York City, held a press briefing at the World Conference Center, and was now watching the sunset at the Long Island estate of the president of the United States. The home of Jessica Mooran.

Punctually, at 8:00, after getting directions from one of the security guards, Cara took her seat in the dining room. Moments later, Tim appeared.

"Good news," he announced as he entered the door. "The president's daughter will be in residence for the remainder of the summer. Security is heaviest when she is present, so I don't think there's a thing to worry about."

"You're right, Mr. Felmar," said Jessica, entering behind him. "Ms. Romero is perfectly safe here with me." She reached forward, switched the place cards on the table and sat in the chair directly opposite Cara.

"Oh good, you're all here," exclaimed Mrs. Anderson, peeking out from the kitchen "I'll begin serving, eh?"

"Why don't you give us a few moments to enjoy our wine," called Jessica, as she picked up the carafe. "May I pour for you, Ms. Romero? Or would you prefer to have Mr. Felmar do it?"

"I would be honored to have you pour. And I would be doubly honored if you would call me Cara."

"And I would feel much more comfortable if you would use Tim, Ms. Mooran."

Delighted to hear the Ms., Cara smiled to herself as she watched Jessica pour the wine. Denim pants and shirt did not distract from the grace of her motions.

"And please call me Jessica," she said resolutely as she finished pouring into her own glass. "Now, I want to hear all about Cali."

The conversation flowed. Jessica, comfortable as hostess, asked about Cali's government, the architecture, the restaurants. Carefully, she refrained from asking about their lifestyles. They could have been talking about England or Australia or any other country. There was no indication of any interest or curiosity about homosexuality. Tim, of course, deferred to Cara on almost all questions, and the table talk had changed to an almost private chatter of conversation between the two women, when Mrs. Anderson interrupted.

"Ms. Jessica," she said, appearing at the dining room entrance, "it's nine p.m. and I must start serving if I am to finish before going to bed."

"Oh, I am sorry. Time just got away from me. Please begin. If you don't finish, don't worry about it. I'll take over. It's just so rare that we have such nice guests." She looked at Cara as she finished speaking. "May I pour some more wine?"

Is the wine corrupting my imagination, thought Cara, *or are those gray eyes glistening sunbeams?* "No, I think I've had quite enough. American wines seem to be stronger than Calian. I don't yet know where my limits are."

"I'm sure you'll find them. You strike me as a quick learner."

Challenged, Cara responded, "That depends upon the teacher."

During dinner, she chastised herself for responding to Jessica's attempts at eye contact. *She's just being polite,* she told herself as she again caught her peering up through lowered lids. *You can't go through America thinking heterosexual women are cruising you.*

"Excellent," declared Tim, as he pushed away his empty plate. "That, Cara, is a much better example of American food than we had last night."

"It was a typical American summer meal," volunteered Jessica. "Clam chowder, barbecued chicken, corn on the cob, and sliced tomatoes. What could be better?"

"Just leave everything where it is," said Mrs. Anderson as she walked past the table, moving hurriedly toward the stairs. "I'll take care of it all in the morning, eh?"

"She's a great old lady," said Jessica as she nodded in the cook's direction. "And a good cook, besides. Speaking of morning, Cara, I often go for an early morning swim this time of year. Do you think you're up to that? It would be nice to have company."

"That sounds good. Very good."

"See you at seven-thirty at the pool then, and I'll look forward to seeing you again tomorrow evening," she said, turning to Tim as the three rose from the table.

"Look forward to seeing me, hell," exclaimed Tim as he and Cara reached the stairs. "She didn't even know I was there." Cara looked back and saw Jessica clearing the table. As they reached the small sitting alcove at the top of the stairs, Tim asked hesitantly, "Can we talk for a few minutes?"

"Sure. What's up?"

"Well, I was wondering. Do you think it would be all right if I left you here alone for a few days? Until Wednesday afternoon when the conference begins. You couldn't be in a safer place and I could use the time to go back to the city to try to find Barbra."

"Oh God, I had completely forgotten about her."

"That doesn't surprise me," he said with a devilish grin.

"I think that would be a wonderful idea."

"I thought you'd like it. But, are you going to be okay?" he added with a more serious expression.

"Absolutely!"

Sixteen

～❦～

It was before 7:00 when Cara quickly ate one of the pastries that had been left for her on the dining room table and exited from the main building. She nodded to the two secret service men standing nearby, licked the crumbs from her fingers, and began walking down the cliffside stairs that led to the swimming pool. She hadn't yet alighted on the second plateau when she realized that her hostess had arrived before her.

Reaching the pool, she quietly slipped into a chaise lounge and watched as Jessica danced her body through the water. She swam with an almost effortless motion, her strokes lacking the purposefulness of a long-distance swimmer. On this occasion, Jessica wore a bathing suit, an adornment that, only because of the circumstances, pleased Cara. But nothing could distract her from the beauty of the dark, lean body as Jessica rolled over to begin back stroking.

"Oh, good, you're here," she exclaimed, her face noticeably brightening as she saw Cara watching her.

She makes my whole body smile, thought Cara as she dove into the pool. Coming up at the other end, she swam several lengths before stopping in front of Jessica who had moved to an underwater seat at the western end of the pool least visible to security personnel.

"I knew you would be a good swimmer. You have a swimmer's body, long and muscular. My dolphins would love you."

"You have your own dolphins?"

"No," she laughed, displaying dimples in the hollows of the high cheeks, "at the marine laboratory. When I'm not on vacation, I'm Doctor Jessica Mooran, in charge of the mammals section of the United States Aquarium."

doi:10.1300/5559_17

"You look much too young for such a prestigious position," commented Cara, visibly impressed.

"I'm only three years younger than you. I'll be twenty-nine next month."

"How did you know my age?" she asked with surprise.

"That's easy. I picked up a press release from Michael Angelico's office when I first learned that you would be visiting. There wasn't enough information, so I wrote to Cali on my father's letterhead and requested your press clippings."

"Jessica," Cara asked hesitantly, "is there a reason for your doing all this research?"

"Not a good one. You sounded much more interesting than I thought a lesbian would be. So, I wanted to know more. Curiosity. Come, let's swim," she said as she pushed off the side of the wall.

They swam side by side for almost a half hour, bodies rhythmically moving through the water, droplets of each other's strokes spraying their faces. They did not speak, continuously swimming. Cara swam as if in a race with her emotions.

Jessica quit first, scampering up the steps and falling onto a chaise. Cara swam for a few more minutes, harder than before, shortening the time between turns, lengthening her strokes, actually picking up speed. *If I swim fast enough,* she thought, *I may outswim my hammering lust.*

Exhausted, she collapsed on the lounge next to Jessica's and lay still listening to the sounds of their labored breathing. Looking over at the motionless body, she watched the light shimmering on the long dark lashes caught in the rays of August's early sun. Curled tightly against the nape of her neck, her dark hair glistened against the copper of unblemished skin, leaving meandering rivulets of water drizzling across her back. *She's like a flower made lovelier by the rain,* thought Cara.

Jessica spoke first. "It is a glorious day, isn't it?"

"Yes."

"I hope you have many days like this while you are visiting us." Her face became pensive as she looked toward a shrub next to the pool. The lovely eyes squinted. "Isn't that a meadowlark?"

She continued without waiting for an answer. "There's an old fable about the meadowlark and Cali that Mrs. Anderson used to tell me when I was very young. Would you like to hear it?"

Cara nodded.

"It seems that right after the great earthquake, all the meadowlarks in this country stopped singing. At first people were very upset, but then, after a while, they got used to it and they stopped listening for the little songstresses. Except for a woman by the name of May Ling whose favorite bird was the meadowlark. She kept listening and listening for the flutelike song. Then one day she was told that her baby would have to be sent to Cali, and she stopped listening because she couldn't hear anything except the sound of her own tears." Jessica put her hands to her face and made motions of wiping her eyes. "She was inconsolable. There was nothing anyone could do to make her stop crying. She just cried and cried. Her husband asked the doctor what to do and the doctor told him to send the infant to Cali as soon as possible so that May Ling would stop crying. But that didn't work. She cried even harder. Finally her husband asked her what would make her stop crying. And she said she would stop only if she got a sign telling her that her baby was happy in Cali. That night, her husband prayed and prayed. And the next morning, a miracle happened. May Ling was sitting in the kitchen crying when suddenly a meadowlark flew in the window and sat on the table in front of her. Shocked, May Ling stopped crying, and just as she did, the meadowlark puffed up its chest, opened its mouth, and began to sing. When the bird finished, May Ling looked at it with tears of joy in her eyes and said, 'I promise to never cry again, if you will tell the meadowlarks to sing whenever they see a happy child in Cali.' And as if by magic, all the meadowlarks throughout the country suddenly began singing. May Ling never cried again, and to this day, the meadowlarks still sing."

She smiled, an inhibited smile of embarrassment, and waited for Cara to comment.

"That's a lovely story. Very sensitive. Very sweet."

"Are the children really happy in Cali? Yesterday, you told me about the country. Today, I would like to know about the people."

She propped herself into a sitting position, prepared to listen attentively. "What's it like growing up in Cali?"

"Really very special. In Cali, there is no such thing as an unwanted
child. Adoptive parents must meet very strict requirements. To pursue the goal of adopting a child, they must want a child very badly.
There are many tests they must pass—psychological, emotional, financial. There are Calians who have been turned down several times,
while there are others who have two or three children. So, our children—who are really your children—are almost always raised in
good, loving homes."

Her gray eyes opened wide. "What about biological children?
Doesn't anyone ever have their own child?"

"The ship goes two ways," answered Cara sadly, knowing that almost no Calian residents could claim Cali as their country of birth.
"Some Calians have had children, through intercourse or fertilization
implants, but our laws are very specific. No one can live in Cali unless
they test positive for the Scarpetti gene. All citizens are randomly
tested for the gene before their sixth birthday. Those who test negative are immediately deported."

Her face openly displaying her confusion, Jessica finally asked, "Isn't
that reverse discrimination?"

"Yes," said Cara politely.

For just the slightest moment, Jessica's face clouded over, and then
she giggled softly, "I guess you're entitled." She stood up and turned
her chaise so that she and Cara would be facing each other. As she
bent over, small beads of perspiration trickled from her navel. *I would
love to lick those beads,* thought Cara. Again sitting, Jessica asked solemnly, "What if the United States reinstituted abortions? How
would that affect your country?"

Cara, hoping her flushed face would not reveal her carnal thoughts,
delayed answering. "The sun is getting quite hot. Let me think about
that while I swim a few laps."

She dove as high and far as she could, feeling the chill spread from
her outstretched hands to her toes. The cold water slapping at her
body felt good. Lazily, she swam, finally stopping at the side of the
pool opposite their chaises. She turned her back to Jessica and looked

out at Long Island Sound. She stayed that way for several minutes, reminding herself that this was the Sound, not the Pacific. This was America, not Cali. This woman, this sensuous woman with the incredible sculptured face was heterosexual.

Returning to Jessica, she lightly dried herself with a beach towel, and continued the conversation. "You asked whether reinstituting abortions would affect my country. That's a yes and no. With the absence of the homosexual constituency that existed before the exodus, I don't think America will ever have enough liberals to again support an abortion law. However, if they did, and if women aborted fetuses because they harbored the Scarpetti gene, my country would pursue a genetic alteration program that would enable Calian women to have gene-positive children so that homosexuals would continue to maintain a balance of ten percent of the world's population. We have the technology available now, but it's highly classified and we will not permit genetic alteration unless we are threatened with extinction."

"What a horrible thought," exclaimed Jessica quickly. "To think that someone as extraordinary as you could even possibly be destroyed because of ignorant prejudices. Come," she said standing up, "I don't want to think about that. Let's go down to the beach. I've brought a picnic basket with nice surprises for lunch."

Eager to feel familiar sand on her feet, Cara jumped up and led the way down the final set of stairs. At the bottom stood two security men.

"I'm wearing a VIP locator that keeps the secret service informed of my exact location at all times," explained Jessica.

"Where could you possibly be hiding a transmitter?" asked Cara as she put her hand out to the security man who helped her down an oversized step that had obviously been battered by the waves and tides. Turning around, she instinctively reached for Jessica who, perceptively, gave her hand and smiled with her eyes.

"The transmitting disc is actually located in the earring of my left ear," she explained as they began walking. "You needn't worry about the security men. We'll be out of their sight in a few minutes."

What a strange thing to say, thought Cara.

The beach felt good. Hot. Familiar. Pure. As they walked, she watched the lazy waters of the sound embracing the shore. *It must be an outgoing tide,* she thought, seeing the valleys of sand being drawn to the sea by the strong undertow. Instantaneously she was reminded of the last lines of a poem she had written some fifteen years earlier— a poem she hadn't thought of since its creation.

> *I love you more than that, as the sea loves the shore;*
> *I cannot love you less, I dare not love you more.*

Was it a prophecy?

They walked almost a mile, Cara enthusiastically picking up treasures. Mostly stones. A few shells of unknown origin. Jessica shared her joy, commenting on each choice, picking up a few of her own. They laughed at the discovery of a hermit crab, kicking and fussing as Cara mistakenly disturbed his morning nap. They smiled at the brightly colored sails out at sea, and at each other.

"This is one of my favorite spots in the whole world," said Jessica as they rounded a bend and reached a beach area that curved inward, interrupting the straight shoreline of cliffs. "It's very private. No one can see us. I call it Jessica's Lair." Her head cocked to one side, she used her hands to emphasize the sense of it all.

"Has anyone ever told you how adorable you are?" Cara asked with a sober expression.

Casting her eyes downward a bit longer than necessary, Jessica reached into the large picnic hamper and removed an oversized towel, spreading it on the ground and placing the basket on top. "Now we can relax," she said as she slipped her forefinger into her black bikini bottom and began slowly sliding the bathing suit down over her hips.

"No," yelled Cara, feeling a catch in her throat as she saw the flash of lighter skin. "I can't allow that." She paused and took a deep breath. "Jessica, I'm a lesbian . . . a homosexual from Cali. You're the president's daughter. We can't be seen together nude."

"Why not?"

"Please," implored Cara, grabbing her wrist. Feeling light-headed, almost dizzy, she held tightly until Jessica finally relaxed her arm.

"I'm sorry. I didn't mean to upset you," she said with an ingenuous expression. "I didn't know how much it mattered to you."

A few unfilled minutes passed between them, Cara wondering whether she had behaved properly. Finally, Jessica spoke in her rich American voice, "Let's eat!"

Going through the picnic basket was a culinary delight. There were several kinds of pâté, salmon salad, whitefish salad, chicken with capers, assorted rolls, desserts of several kinds, and a variety of herbal teas. Cara, realizing she was hungry, ate with her customary zeal, chattering between bites about the food in Cali.

"I love to watch you," said Jessica, gazing at her through sun squinted eyes. "You're so alive. So vibrant. You must have been raised by wonderful people."

"And what about you?" asked an embarrassed Cara. "You know all about me. Now tell me about you."

"There's not much. My mother died in a car accident when I was five. I was raised by Mrs. Anderson who had been with the family before I was born. I have no brothers. No sisters. I love working with dolphins. And I love being on the beach, nude." She grinned.

And Cara knew it was all right. Those gray teasing eyes told her so.

It was almost 5:00 when they finally returned to the house. Showering outdoors, still in their bathing suits, she watched as Jessica lathered her limber body and wondered if she could survive three weeks in a state of perpetual lust. When Jessica dropped the soap and bent to pick it up, her petite form touching Cara's, she felt her heart cry.

"Will you be joining me for dinner tonight?" Cara asked, avoiding eye contact.

"Of course," she said emphatically, nodding her thanks as Cara scurried to open the door to the main house. "At eight."

—❦—

Rummaging through her meager American wardrobe, she finally settled on a dinner outfit of pale blue pants and matching blouse. Not because of their cut or style, which was really rather dull, but because the color called attention to her eyes while contrasting with the richness of her soft blonde hair.

Standing before the full wall mirror, brushing her hair into an assortment of styles, she spoke to herself admonishingly. "This is a heterosexual woman who has absolutely no interest in you other than friendship. And that, dear self, should be your only interest in her. Stop playing with fire!" Finally, after spending thirty minutes arranging her hair into a perfect French twist, she started out of the room, begrudgingly stopped, turned around and snarled at herself in the mirror. "You're a tough disciplinarian," she muttered as she removed the pins and let her hair flow loose.

The dining room was empty, giving Cara a few meditative moments alone to admire the spectacular view of the August sunset, glowing pink over the dimming waters. Mesmerized, she had difficulty averting her eyes from the kaleidoscope of color when Jessica excitedly plopped a stack of newspapers on the table in front of her. "Look at this!" she yelled excitedly. "The American press never gives anyone this much attention. Not even my father!" Leaning over her shoulder, she read the headlines aloud as Cara leafed through the papers. "'Cali Utopia Says Lesbian,' 'Lesbian Speaks Out,' and this one is the best, 'Stunning Lesbian Stuns Press.'" *Sherry Ryan gets the thanks for that one,* thought Cara as she read the byline.

"Ms. Jessica, I heard those dishes clatter. You'd better be careful or you're gonna break a place setting," said Mrs. Anderson, bustling out of the kitchen. "Do you want me to start serving now?"

"Yes, please." Hugging Cara from behind, placing her cheek next to hers, pressing tightly, Jessica chattered on. "I'm just so proud of you. When I first saw that press kit, I knew you would take this country by storm." Suddenly, she stepped back, a flush of crimson highlighting the copper cheeks. "Is it okay to hug you? It is okay, isn't it?"

"Of course," she smiled, wishing there was a way to inject someone with the Scarpetti gene.

Jumping up again, Jessica walked to the sideboard, returning with a set of gold candleholders and two delicately tapered candles. "This calls for a celebration. These are part of the Hargreaves collection. I think we should light them tonight in your honor."

Putting the newspapers aside so that Mrs. Anderson could set down her dinner salad, Cara turned back to see Jessica's gray eyes dancing with the reflection of the twinkling flame. Unnerved by the hug, and now the intimacy of a candlelit dinner, she cleared her throat and tried diverting attention to a more formal conversation. "What is the Hargreaves collection?"

"It's a collection of the more than seven thousand pieces that Ellyn Hargreaves left behind. I documented and catalogued each piece when my father became president. Then, through diplomatic channels, I contacted her to see if there was anything she wanted. I really thought it would be the entire collection. There were so many beautiful pieces, like these solid gold candleholders." She paused, tenderly tracing the ornate base with her hand. "But all she wanted was a small book of sonnets by somebody named Jane Mitchell."

She waited for Cara to respond, but when no response was forthcoming, she continued, "Did you know Jane Mitchell? Was she a special part of her life?"

"Yes, very."

"Oh?"

"She was her sister. She died in a car crash several years ago," Cara answered coldly.

"I'm sorry. I thought it may have been a . . . a lover."

"I know what you thought," said Cara abruptly. "I'm sorry if I disappointed you."

"No. . . . Yes. Yes, I am disappointed, but only because I've spent the last couple of years daydreaming that they had a wonderfully romantic relationship. I even fantasized about the love songs she wrote for Jane." She looked at Cara with an expression that tore at her heart. "I didn't mean to offend you."

It was several minutes before Cara spoke. "The candles are lovely. I will tell Ellyn that I shared them with you."

"Do you and Ellyn Hargreaves know one another well?" she hesitatingly asked.

"Yes, very well."

"I think I'm jealous," she confessed, gray eyes peering directly at Cara.

Of which one of us, Cara wondered.

Later that night, her concentration affected by thoughts of the day's adventures, Cara took an indeterminably long time reading the newspapers. Finally finishing, she turned to the television, dialed the newscasts, and watched all the primary reports of the previous forty-eight hours. To her surprise, most stations carried the full press briefing. She was delighted with the results. If there was a criticism, it was that she had come across as a bit chauvinistic, but why not? *Calians,* she thought, *had a right to be chauvinistic.* She fell asleep with the television on. Her last thoughts were of Jessica.

Seventeen

For the next three days the two women of contrasting beauty were inseparable, almost all of their waking hours spent in each other's company.

They swam, talked, felt the sun on their backs, smiled incessantly, walked endless hours on the beach, and listened to the sound of the meadowlark. Picnics at Jessica's Lair, a daily afternoon activity, extended into the sunset hour when they would finally wander back, exhausted, two silhouettes against a darkening sky.

After dinner, Cara would sit in the kitchen in an old-fashioned caned chair with her feet propped up on the stove while Jessica washed the evening dishes that Mrs. Anderson never finished. They spoke and laughed, but mainly they felt—the deep saturated feelings of a friendship being born.

Ellyn Hargreaves, whose music they both loved, became their constant companion. They programmed her old compact discs onto Cara's watch and brought them to the pool and the Lair and on their walks. At night, they sat together on the surround-sound couch in the entertainment room, filling the air with Ellyn's renditions of the old-fashioned love songs. Sometimes Jessica would lay her head on Cara's shoulder and Cara's heart would swell to infinite proportions. *Will I ever again know such happiness?* she asked herself.

On Monday afternoon, their routine changed when Jessica asked her to help her shop for clothes in one of the local boutiques. "I'm so envious every time I think of you in that wonderful Calian outfit. You have such a good sense of style."

Waiting in the sitting room, Cara commented enthusiastically on each of the eight outfits she modeled. A short pale pink dress garnered particular applause, inspiring Jessica to curtsy. "You are so good for

doi:10.1300/5559_18

my ego. Now, if you will do me the favor of unzipping me, I will end your torture and reward you with an ice cream cone."

Behind them, two saleswomen who had obviously recognized Cara, stood with their heads together whispering feverishly.

"Oh, don't worry about them," laughed Jessica, arching her left eyebrow in the expression that tickled the hairs on the back of Cara's neck. "They've seen my body before and they won't be the least bit jealous."

"You are so bad," whispered Cara, as her trembling hands grazed the silky skin.

After a short stroll while eating an ice cream cone, they returned to the estate, Jessica baffled by her feelings of disappointment that they wouldn't be taking an afternoon outdoor shower together.

"Dinner at the same time?" asked Cara when they reached the stairs.

"Not for me. I almost forgot to tell you. I'll be having dinner with my fiancé tonight. There's a museum benefit and I promised weeks ago that I'd go with him." She hesitated before speaking again in a soft voice that threatened to become a whisper. "But I'd really much rather stay here with you." And she turned around and walked up the stairs as though nothing unusual had been said.

Eighteen

—❦❦❦—

"So, you'll be dining alone tonight, Ms. Romero, eh?" asked Mrs. Anderson as she took her place at the table.

"I guess so. Mr. Felmar is in the city and Ms. Mooran is attending a museum benefit, so I'll have to enjoy your cooking all by myself."

"Well, you needn't be bored while ya do it. I've saved today's *Modern Woman* magazine for you. There's a really nice article about your visit to this country."

"Good heavens," exclaimed Cara to a beaming Mrs. Anderson. "I had no idea that the United States would give me quite this much attention."

"I'm real proud of you, Ms. Romero. Real proud," she said emphatically as she walked over to the table and picked up Cara's hand, delicately wrapping it in her own pudgy fingers. "I've read every one of those articles, and there isn't one that you can't be proud of. That speech was really something, and it's about time this country learned something about Cali. Our government, and that means President Mooran too, doesn't want us to know anything, eh? They don't want us to know that maybe they made a mistake thirty-five years ago."

"And you, Mrs. Anderson," she asked sincerely, "do you think the United States made a mistake?"

"I know they did. I was in my thirties when it all happened. I saw those people going nuts. Blaming homosexuals for everything. Like they were responsible for all the things that were going wrong in this country. And those preachers! Showing dirty pictures every time you turned on the TV. All they wanted was money. Fools! We were fools to allow our children to be taken from us." She paused, releasing Cara's hand that she had been patting affectionately.

"Did you lose any children to Cali?"

"No. Never had any. I was married for only a couple of years. A lazy man, he was. Ended in divorce. I've been working for the Moorans for thirty-four years. But my first cousin, a nice man by the name of Gerald, he went over on the very first ship. In 2020. He was a carpenter. The best darn carpenter I ever knew. He never did anybody any harm. But," she smiled, "I bet he's happy now. I guess in the long run, the exodus was a good thing for your people, eh?"

"I guess it was. Yes, I guess it was."

"Well, I'd better move on and serve you some dinner," she said, walking toward the kitchen, "or you'll be replacing Ms. Jessica as my scullery maid." She chuckled. "It's a little game we play. Almost every night when dinner is delayed, I tell Ms. Jessica that I'll take care of the dishes in the morning. And in the morning, when I come down, the dishes are always done. She's my darlin' little leprechaun, that one!"

A tinge of jealousy passed through Cara. The possessive expression of endearment awakened an emotion she hadn't felt in a long time. It hurt. In less than four days, the idea of sharing Jessica had already become painful. You've got it bad, she admonished herself. Instinctively, she ran her fingers through the wayward shock of hair that fell across her forehead.

Reviewing some material for the conference, she had fallen asleep still fully clothed when she was awakened at midnight by the noise of the wind clattering past the open balcony door. Quietly, she got up and closed it, and without hesitation, walked softly across the hall to Tim's room.

Entering his suite, she crossed to his balcony and peered out the glass to the spot where the limousine had been parked. Jessica had not yet returned. An hour later, she had almost decided to go back to her room when she saw the car emerge from the moonlit forest. Spellbound, she watched as an exquisite Jessica stepped from the car. Dressed in a short white gown, she appeared even more breathtaking in the moonlight than Cara's imagination had allowed her to fantasize. Exiting behind her was a shorter replica of Tim. They put their heads together, discussing something he had said. Transfixed by the activity, she continued to stare, feeling her heart plummet to an undetermined spot. She watched them kiss, grateful that it was not long and lingering. When he reentered the waiting limousine Cara almost cheered.

"Now, maybe I can go back to sleep," she said aloud as she noiselessly returned to her room.

Nineteen

—◅◈▻—

Tuesday morning sunlight streamed into her room through the balcony door. *That'll teach you,* she thought, when she realized that in her haste to get to bed after returning from Tim's room she had forgotten to pull the drapes closed. She lay in bed, not quite awake, and watched the dust dance in the hazy yellow beams. Stretching with joy, she softly whispered in a singsong voice, "She didn't have sex with him. She didn't have sex with him."

She forced herself to stay in bed until 7:00 a.m., and when she could no longer possess her soul in patience, she jumped up, showered, put on her bathing suit, gathered her beach towel, and raced down to the swimming pool, almost knocking over a maid who was trying to enter the house.

Adrift in the pool, propelled by the pink mist, was a yellow chair float, an indication that someone had been there before her, but Jessica was nowhere to be seen. It surprised Cara that security people were allowed to use the pool, but thinking no more about it, she dove in and climbed into the seat. Closing her eyes, she leaned back and thought about the glorious day ahead. It was to be their last full day together before the conference. They would picnic again, she supposed. Or perhaps play tennis. Were there stables? Maybe they could go riding. But it was the idea of a picnic that pleased her most of all. She liked being close to Jessica. The occasional touch of that lovely hand, even if only in narrative gestures, made her smile.

By 10:00 she had tired of sunbathing and swimming. Disappointed by Jessica's continued absence, she went down to the beach and asked one of the security men if they had seen her. Obligingly, he pulled out his monitor, no bigger than a business card, and squeezed

doi:10.1300/5559_20

it several times. A few seconds later, it emitted a series of musical notes. "Nope. She didn't get by me. She's not on the beach."

"Do you know where she is?"

He nodded politely. "Yes ma'am, the monitor just told me, but I'm not allowed to give out that kind of information. I'm sorry."

"That's okay," she said as she began to walk in a westerly direction. After only a few steps, she decided that it was a great day for a work-out and broke into a slow run. Long Island Sound looked like strings of diamonds dancing on blue silk, the sand was firm, and she needed to clear her head of Jessica.

"I can't believe she's a lesbian," muttered the security man under his breath as he watched the long blonde hair waving in the wind, rhythmically matching the effortless strides of her long lean body. "She's a beauty. Looks just like an all-American beauty."

"What's that you're saying, Bob?" asked his partner walking up alongside of him.

"I sure wish she wasn't a lesbian."

"Yeah," he chuckled, "you and a few million other Americans."

She ran a few feet past the Lair, smiling to herself in reminiscence of their first picnic, then turned and stopped to sit for a few minutes. Stretching her body against the coolness of the grass, she considered removing her bathing suit which had dried too quickly in the morning sun when she thought she heard a noise. A sound, barely audible to one without martial arts sensitivity training, abruptly stopped her from making any further movements. With little motion, she cast her eyes to the left. Seeing nothing, she slowly circled to the right. There, in her direct line of vision, not more than fifteen yards from her head, she saw the doe with her twin fawns.

It's magic, thought Cara, who had never seen a white-tailed deer. Moving only her eyes, she watched the fawns cavort in the high grass, springing up, racing forth, chasing, while the doe, ears alert, ignored them and pulled at the berries on the nearby shrubs. Losing interest in the game, the smallest fawn tried nursing on its mother, who gently nudged it away with her nose while licking its ears and neck. Walking slowly, oblivious to Cara's presence, the doe moved around the bend, quickly followed by the two little ones.

Sitting up, she smiled at the disappearing white tail of the fawn. "I've been nurtured," she exclaimed aloud.

It was past noon when she entered the dining room of the main house. "I'm hungry. I forgot to pick up a pastry this morning," she said to Mrs. Anderson, who was by herself in the dining area. "Will I be eating alone?"

"I think so. Ms. Jessica went for a very early morning swim. Had a late breakfast, she did. I don't think she'll be having any lunch today. But I have the perfect cure for your hunger. Maine lobster salad on a hard roll with sliced tomatoes and slaw on the side. How's that for your gurgling belly?"

"Sounds good to me," she responded, thinking about the pool float and the body who must have sat in it before her.

"You know, Ms. Romero," said the likable housekeeper as Cara was finishing her last crumbs, "if you don't have any special plans for this afternoon, you might want to go down to the workout room. It's in the basement. Fully equipped with the latest stuff, I hear. Might be a nice way for you to spend the day, eh?"

Thanking Mrs. Anderson, Cara decided to return to her room first to change clothes and rest the recommended half hour before heavy physical activity. Diverting herself from thoughts of Jessica, she purposefully telephoned Vanessa who had promised to spend most nights in Cara's apartment. She's probably screwing her brains out about now, she grinned as she looked at her watch and saw it was 10:30 a.m. in Cali.

After punching in her special diplomat's code on the phone monitor, she turned off the visual and waited for Vanessa to answer.

"Anisette's residence," said the husky voice at the other end.

"Don't you allow that cat to take over my apartment. She controls enough already," laughed Cara.

"She took over your apartment a long time ago, baby doll. You just haven't realized it yet."

"Sounds like the two of you are getting along well."

"One of us is . . . and it's not me," yelled Vanessa trying to drown out a purring Anisette who was rubbing her face against the phone.

"Now that I've assured you that your oldest child is well and sassy, I think I'll put her in a closet and get back to my favorite breakfast."

Hearing a woman's laughter in the background, Cara's face suddenly reddened. "I can't believe you said that on a diplomatic phone line."

"What's the matter, don't you think Americans do it?"

No more calls for now, decided Cara, as she laughingly turned off the phone, and changed into shorts and a tank top. *It's time to sweat.*

Eager to see the equipment, she resolutely pushed open the door to the gym and almost tripped when she found herself looking directly at Jessica peddling an exercise bicycle.

As though intruding on Jessica's privacy, she started to back out, thought better of it, marched in, put her towel down and mounted the bicycle alongside her. "It was a beautiful morning for the beach. I'm sorry I missed you." When she barely nodded, only glancing in her direction, Cara continued, "I went to your lair and was visited by a doe with her two fawns. They were entertaining, but it wasn't as entertaining as being with you."

Staring straight ahead, Jessica finally spoke in a polite, unemotional voice. "I awakened very early this morning and decided to go for a swim before breakfast. I've been working out ever since."

Peddling hard, trying to match her speed, Cara was having difficulty maintaining the rapid pace. Several times she adjusted the pedal pressure, but could not keep up. "Will you be having dinner with me tonight? Or am I being punished for something?" she asked in the encompassing silence.

Waiting an indeterminate time, she never took her eyes from Jessica's proud profile. The bottom lip quivered and Cara thought she was going to respond, but instead, she jumped off the bicycle, ignoring the spinning pedals, and moved quickly for the door. Leaping after her, Cara reached out and turned her around so they were facing each other squarely. "Wait! At least tell me what I've done wrong. Is it something I did? Something I said?" She looked down at the troubled gray eyes. "Talk to me, damn it!"

"Last night, I told Roland I could no longer see him."

"Why? Why did you do that?" Breathing rapidly, she grabbed Jessica by the shoulders, gently pinning her against the closed door. "Why?"

"Because I'm falling in love with you," she shouted angrily.

Feeling her knees tremble, Cara relaxed her grip, slumping against the wall. Her voice was barely audible. "That's impossible. This can't be."

"Right!" she responded as she walked out the door.

Sitting on the bench, running her hands through her hair, Cara was immobile for several minutes. An urgency of thoughts passed through her head. Something was terribly wrong. This could not be happening.

Overwhelmed by the need to feel familiar territory, she left the house through a side door and went down to the beach. Ignoring the security man she had spoken to earlier in the day, she began walking in an easterly direction, deliberately away from Jessica's Lair. When she reached the boundary of the estate, she sat down in the sand and stared at the sea, searching for answers. She sat motionless for the remainder of the afternoon, but came no closer to an understanding than when she began.

Feeling her energy return, she removed her shorts and her tank top, piling them neatly on the sand, and dove into the surf. On the beach, a security woman who Cara had noticed that morning walked over, checked her clothing and sat down and watched the waters.

Tiring more quickly than she had anticipated, she turned over and floated on her back, feeling the rhythm of the gentle waves calming her trembling soul. She thought about the prime minister who had put Cara's name in nomination for this assignment. Had she let her down? Had she disgraced her country?

She squinted at the sky, growing dimmer with the approaching sunset and tried to sort the facts. She was in love with Jessica. Of that, she was sure. But, knowing Jessica was heterosexual, she had been very careful not to encourage physical contact, even withholding the customary expressions of affection she naturally extended to her friends. She had asked nothing of her, made no allusions to sexuality, and encouraged conversations about the men in her life. She had anticipated that she, herself, would be inadvertently hurt by this futile love for a heterosexual, but accepted that as the price for Jessica's passing friendship. Where had things gone wrong, and was she responsible?

And Jessica's anger. Where was that coming from? Did she blame Cara? Did she fear that she would have to go to Cali? Surely, she knew better. During their discussions Cara had repeatedly explained that only people with the Scarpetti gene were allowed into Cali. Was she afraid? Had she read those books written in the 1930s and 1940s about the "love that dared not speak its name?"

And what about now? What would happen now?

Feeling the air getting cold against her exposed skin, she began swimming back to shore, surprised at how far she had drifted. Stroking strongly against the current, she felt better when she was once again able to see the security woman, now standing in the moonlight. Spotting Cara, the woman spoke into her transmitter, then unobtrusively receded into the shadows.

Crawling from the surf, Cara remained on her hands and knees, gasping deeply as the incoming tide nipped at her toes. Several minutes passed before she was able to retrieve her clothing. Dressing quickly, she huddled on the sand, trying to slow her uncontrollable shivers before attempting the long walk back. *I almost became a heroine of one of those 1940s novels,* she speculated sardonically.

It was past 10:00 p.m. when she finally reached the house. Too late, she decided, to even apologize to Mrs. Anderson for missing dinner, she went directly to her room, enjoyed a long, lingering shower, and dragged herself to bed. Channeling her watch to music, she fell asleep to the heartrending sounds of Ellyn Hargreaves.

At 2:00 a.m., awakened by the sound of the surf through the open window, she lay on her side and patiently waited, wistfully following the moonlight as it paved a path across the waters.

Several minutes later, she arose, crossed the bedroom, and opened the door.

"You knew I would come," faintly whispered Jessica, who had barely touched the knob.

"Yes," she said softly as she reached for her hand and gently led her to the bed. Bathed in the night's light, looking more seductive than she had ever thought possible, Cara gaped in wonder at her karma, her sensibilities heightened by the erotic rush that echoed in every crevice of her being. *Let this be sweet and wondrous,* she begged silently as she tenderly removed the robe that sat lightly on Jessica's shoulders.

"Are you sure?" Cara asked before she dared to touch her.

"Yes," she answered. "Very sure."

Reaching out with her hand, she felt Jessica tremble as she began to trace the outline of her body, the fluid lines that flowed so gracefully beneath the silken skin. When she reached a spot whose sensitivity threatened to scream, she bent forth and kissed it before moving on to the next. The rhythm of the tremors grew more erratic and she knew Jessica was ready. Lovingly, Cara brushed her eyes closed with her tongue, and gently parted her lips, kissing her deeply, inhaling her sweet odor of lust. Pressing their bodies together, skin on skin, they kissed again and again and when she was sure that Jessica was beyond pain, she lowered herself, spreading Jessica's labia apart, first with her hand, and then with her tongue. She flitted quickly from spot to spot, holding Jessica's imploring hands with her own. When she was sure that Jessica could endure no longer, she hastened the rhythm on the clitoris, feeling it stiffen and swell beneath her touch. As Jessica's body arched to threatening heights, Cara plunged with her tongue and came in unison, the two of them thrashing in pleasure to the sound of the pounding sea.

They made love again and again, caressing, touching, exploring, kissing, searching. . . . Jessica, tentatively at first, but then with greater and greater intensity, demandingly, until Cara, soaring to peaks never before experienced, cried aloud for her to stop.

"Was I a good lover?" she asked shyly when their bodies finally lay motionless, her head resting on Cara's shoulder.

"For a beginner."

"You shit," she grinned. "I guess I'll just have to keep practicing."

"How about every night for the next seventeen?"

"And then?" she asked after too long a pause.

"And then, ten days of separation, and I return to New York for the one-week conference follow-up for legislative personnel. And now, no more 'and thens,' we both have a big day tomorrow." Brushing the black ringlets with her lips, she held Jessica until she felt her rhythmic breaths of sleep. Summoning her own mind to a blank, she finally joined her, her body curled around Jessica's in a question mark.

Twenty

It was after 10:00 when Cara entered the dining room on Wednesday morning. Jessica had left earlier for the conference center to meet with the presidential press assistant to review the welcoming speech. There was little left for Cara to do except shower and prepare for the afternoon's activities. She had thought about taking a swim, decided she might drown, and chose to begin the day with a self-cooked breakfast instead. Walking into the kitchen, she was startled to find Tim doing the same thing.

"Well, it's about time you showed up," he scolded jokingly as he put the second breakfast package into the cookery machine.

"Tim, welcome back. I'm glad to see you." Stepping on her tiptoes, she kissed him lightly on the cheek. "What happened in the city? Any word on Barbra?"

"Lots of leads, but no action. I'll tell you about it over breakfast," he responded as he turned around and hugged her to his broad chest, taking note of her tan and her radiance.

Sitting over their trays at the dining room table, Tim related his adventures of the previous five days. After leaving the estate at midday on Friday, he went directly to a New York City gay bar that he had learned about from Brian Rayford before departing from Cali. The quaint 1900s-type tavern, called "Stonehenge," catered to those homosexuals who had chosen not to emigrate to Cali during the initial exodus. Although the United States had passed laws criminalizing homosexual relationships, gays could not be stopped from congregating, so there sprang up a network of dingy underground bars that catered to the elderly, dwindling gay population. Stonehenge was the best known in the New York area.

Initially, the Stonehenge treated Tim badly, the patrons fearful of a stranger so much younger than themselves. However, after he presented his identification as a citizen of Cali and answered their questions about some of the celebrities who had fled during the exodus, their tongues loosened and they referred him to Dr. Helena Wordell in the borough of Queens who conducted a private practice catering to gays only, theorizing that if anyone would know Barbra Weissman, it would be a lesbian physician.

Arriving in Queens after Wordell's office had already closed for the day, Tim trekked back to the city, staying at a transient hotel where he knew his identity would not be questioned. To prevent any suspicion about him being in contact with American citizens for nondiplomatic purposes, he spent the weekend in his room, venturing out only for meals. "I'll tell you, Cara," he complained, "I thought about you back here safely in the luxury of this estate with a view of the sound and Mrs. Anderson's cooking and concluded that I must be crazy."

On Monday, he returned to the doctor's office, informing the receptionist that he had been referred to Dr. Wordell because of pains in his ears. "Her answer made me feel like a jerk." He chuckled. "She answered, 'Well, ears should be interesting—Dr. Wordell is a proctologist and treats problems of the rectum only.' I told her that she must have misunderstood me, because I had said that I was having pains in my ass."

Laughing until the tears rolled down, Tim stopped to regain his breath before finishing the story. After entering Wordell's office, he explained to her that he was looking for a woman physician named Barbra Weissman. Attempting to allay Wordell's suspicions and especially her fears of the Olms, he told her that Barbra had been very kind to Brian Rayford when she had treated him eight years earlier and he had given Tim a gift to pass on to her. Searching through her computerized medical directories, Wordell was able to give him no concrete information. The only thing she could tell him was that she had heard a rumor about three months before that there was a new lesbian doctor working for the United States government out of a New York City office.

He spent the rest of Monday and all day Tuesday trying to ferret out more information from the various government offices. To no avail.

"But I'm sure that Wordell's rumor is correct and that the new lesbian doctor is Barbra. It all fits. She's been missing from the *Fantasia* for about three months and she does work for the government."

"So, what are you going to do next?" she asked, licking her fingers after wiping up the last of her gooey eggs with a piece of rye toast.

"There's still two weekends left when you'll be safely ensconced in this palatial splendor, so I thought I'd use those days to continue my search in the hell holes of New York. . . . I'm not complaining, of course."

"Of course." She smiled.

"Now tell me," he asked, as he pushed away his tray and leaned back in the chair, his big body causing it to perch precariously on two legs, "what's been happening with you? Do I perceive some changes in your life?"

Realizing that her relationship with Jessica would be impossible to hide from Tim, she related the events of the past several days. "So, that's where it's at . . . everywhere, yet nowhere," she said despairingly at the completion of the story. In the silence that followed, she felt herself looking a bit too defiantly at Tim. Casting her eyes downward, she rose from the table, circled round and stood at his back, glaring out the window that overlooked the sound. "Are you ashamed of me?" she spat out.

"No . . . no. Of course not." He pivoted in his chair to look at her. "I'm just shocked. This is going to take a little getting used to." He sat silently for a few moments, then slapped his hand on his knee in a gesture of discontent. "I don't get it. I just don't get it. All this talk about the Scarpetti gene. How can this—"

"Tim, I did nothing to mislead Jessica or to seduce her in any way. I was very careful—"

"Cara," he interrupted as he stood and hugged her to him, gently patting her on the back as one would a child, "I'm not suggesting you did anything dishonorable. I don't know you very well, but I certainly know you well enough to know that much. But there is something wrong." Stepping back, he looked at her with an earnest expression. "Is it possible that Jessica is experimenting? Or that she's simply curious and looking for a juicy story to share with her upper-crust friends? Is this something for them to laugh about after we leave?"

"No!" Realizing she had responded almost too quickly, almost defensively, she tried to organize her thoughts before speaking further. She looked directly at him and spoke slowly. "I'm very much in touch with my feelings, Tim. I love Jessica. Of that I have no doubt. And, incredible as it seems, she loves me. There are no doubts there either. As to the whys or hows . . . I have no answers. I'm as mystified as you are."

"Do you suppose it's possible for persons without the Scarpetti gene to enter into homosexual relationships?" As Cara began to shake her head, he put up his hand, "Wait, let me finish this thought. In Cali, we would have no statistics on heterosexual behaviors, but there might be some data on this in the United States. As long as I'm going to be visiting government health facilities this weekend, let's see if I can find out anything that would be helpful." He hesitated before continuing. "Don't get your hopes up, but I'll also try to find out if there's such a thing as a false negative result for the Scarpetti gene. Maybe it's possible that Jessica tested negative in error."

"Thanks, Tim."

"For what?" he asked.

"For being Tim Felmar."

Twenty-One

The weekend arrived much too quickly. Although Cara was anxious to again spend days with Jessica, she mourned the rapid passage of time. The first three days of the conference had been interesting. Jessica's speech, delivered in her wonderful resonant voice, was well received by the participants, especially Cara. The meetings had been well attended and, as expected, a great deal of attention was given to Cali's accomplishments in the care of the elderly. Time and again Cara was called upon to provide data, debate issues, and offer advice. Although the conference was only in its first week, it had already been made clear that Cali was the acknowledged leader in the field of aging, and Cara the respected expert.

But it was not the days that were special to Cara. It was the nights and the time spent with Jessica. She couldn't wait to return home each evening and run to her room where Jessica sat waiting. Together, they would spend a few hours walking the beach or talking by the swimming pool. Then they would have a quick dinner with Tim, and go back to her room for another wondrous night of lovemaking.

"You're right, Cara," said Tim as they had left that Friday for the conference, "this is not Jessica's fodder for gossip. She really does love you." He and Jessica had become good friends on the first night of his return when he had shown his support for their relationship by suggesting that they plan their evenings without him. "I prefer to spend my time alone," he explained to Mrs. Anderson. Although the two women were grateful to Tim for enabling them to spend their evenings in privacy, they still missed the special daylight moments and long hours the weekend would provide.

On Saturday morning, Tim was departing for New York City at the same time that Jessica was leaving for the beach. "What a difference in lifestyles," he sighed. "You go to the beach and I go to the city. And on such a pretty August day. There's something wrong with this picture."

"Are you sure you don't want to stay and join us?" she asked teasingly.

"Do you really mean that?" he responded, putting down his luggage and standing with his hands on his hips and a big grin on his face. "I can, if you really want me to."

"No!" she smiled over her shoulder as she continued out the door.

Entering the main room, a few minutes behind Jessica, Cara spotted him just as he was about to get into the limousine. "Wait!" she yelled through the open window, stopping him as he reached for the door. Catching up, she led him out of earshot of the driver. "Tim, I know Jessica is not heterosexual," she insisted. "I'd bet my life on it. When you visit the government agencies, please do some careful research on that possibility of a false negative Scarpetti test. And whatever you find out, do not share the information with Jessica. Until we've had a chance to consider all the options—if there are any options—I don't want to upset her."

"You're the boss. Whatever you want me to do is fine with me."

After watching the limousine enter the forest, she ran down the stairs and joined Jessica on the beach. "To the Lair!" Cara yelled and the two women ran, matching strides, in the heavy sand. Shrugging shoulders at their exuberance, the security men sat down on the bench in anticipation of a long boring day.

"No fair. I was carrying the picnic basket," said Jessica as she arrived a few seconds behind Cara and fell to the ground beside her.

"Whoever said I was fair?" she asked as she leaned over and pushed Jessica onto her back, kissing her gently on the lips. "And this is something I've always wanted to do," she murmured as she used her tongue to lick the droplets of perspiration that lingered in the sweet cleft.

Their faces only inches apart, Cara was able to see the flash of moisture in Jessica's eyes as she assumed a more somber expression. "You know I love you, Cara."

"Yes. And I . . . you. I loved you the very first time you caught me on my hands and knees." She lightly ran her fingers on Jessica's midriff. "That must have been a sign," she laughed.

Pulling Cara down on top of her, she whispered in her ear, "I want to make love. Here. Now."

"No!" she said sharply, pulling back into a sitting position. "We can't take the chance."

After a few seconds of silence, Jessica jumped to her feet and spread the picnic blanket on the ground, emptying the basket of the sandwiches and snacks she had prepared earlier that morning. "How about a swim before lunch?" she asked, grabbing Cara's hand and pulling her to a standing position.

Later, after they had finished swimming and picnicking and were lying on their backs, hands casually touching, she softly asked, "What's going to happen to us?"

Cara, afraid to look at her, didn't move, her eyes closed in the direction of the sky. "Lots of special things. I will return to Cali and look back upon these times in awe. You, my heart, will probably marry and have two children and a wonderful husband who will love you deeply, though not half as deeply as I."

"That's not good enough," she shouted angrily, coming to a sitting position. "I don't want you to go back to Cali and I don't want a husband." She pulled up a handful of grass and threw it back at the ground. "Stay here with me. Become an American citizen."

Cara took her hands, and held them between her own "You know that's not possible. This country has strict laws against homosexuality. America would never grant me citizenship. Not even your father could change that." She held her hands tighter. "And I wouldn't want it changed. Jessica, I was exiled by this country before you were even born. My country is Cali. It's a country where I can be who I am, where I can live and love openly, where I can kiss your sweet face on the beach without fear of being imprisoned or beaten. You're asking me to give up my freedom. I cannot do that."

A pall of gloom hung over the rest of the day. Jessica was especially despondent. At dinner, even Mrs. Anderson took notice. "I don't know what's the matter with you two young girls, eh? You're picking at your dinner like you don't like my cooking." Going into the kitchen, she returned carrying a covered cake plate. "Well, I know you're going to feel a lot better when you see this. I made a special peach pie with a homemade crust. But you're going to have to save a piece for Mr. Tim for tomorrow, eh? It wouldn't be fair not to."

Politely, both women ate a piece of pie, but their spirits remained unchanged. "Let's take a moonlit walk on the beach," urged Cara as they left the dining room.

"No," mumbled Jessica, "I think I'm beyond consolation." Taking Cara's hand, oblivious to the stunned expression of Mrs. Anderson, she squeezed it affectionately. "I need to be alone tonight to do some serious thinking." Turning back, as an afterthought, she whispered, "I love you."

Twenty-Two

Jumping on Cara's bed, it was evident that Jessica's mood had changed by the next morning. "Wake up so I can tell you how much I love you," she yelled, covering Cara's face with kisses.

"How much?" Throwing off the comforter, she pulled Jessica on top of her. "This much?" Cara asked as she removed Jessica's robe and slid her fingers into the moistening crevice of Jessica's vagina, the fingertips of her left hand lightly riding the hills and valleys of her backbone. It was an hour later before they lay quietly, facing each other with the sweet smiles of the aftermath of lovemaking.

"I've decided to return to Cali with you after your final week in this country," she casually announced as they showered after a late day swim. Lathering her legs with unusual care, she peered up at Cara with the impish expression that was proving so endearing. "And that's that."

Grabbing her towel off the outdoor bench, Cara ran after Jessica into the house and up to her room. "That's not that," she said as she nervously ran her hand through the familiar shock of hair. Pulling off her wet bathing suit, she took both their suits and threw them on the bathroom floor, returning quickly to sit on the bed next to Jessica. "The only way you can get into Cali is by testing positive for the Scarpetti gene. You don't have the gene or you would have been sent to Cali before your third birthday."

"We'll just have to lie. We'll doctor my records. As the daughter of the president I have access to all kinds of people. Nobody will ever know."

"Yes, they will." Frustrated, Cara began pacing the floor. "It's an unusual situation, but I know that my country will insist on testing you right after you enter and that would end the masquerade right

 doi:10.1300/5559_23

there." She paused, breathing deeply before continuing. "Jessica, there are some possibilities that Tim and I are working on, but you must realize the full implications. If we are able to obtain admittance for you to Cali, and you decide to go, it would mean giving up everything and everyone you've ever known. Your life would be totally different."

"But that's the point. It would be the life I'm supposed to have. I don't know why . . . and I don't know how . . . but I do know that I belong with you, and with Tim, and with Jody, and Miriam Ekstrom, and Vanessa, and all the others you talk about. I love my father and Mrs. Anderson," she explained as she stood by the balcony door, her near-perfect body silhouetted against the evening sky, "but I also need to be who I am. And I am Jessica Mooran, the lover of Cara Romero. I belong in Cali with her."

"Oh God, what am I going to do with you?"

"Just love me," said Jessica, burying her head in Cara's shoulder.

Two hours later, after pleasing Mrs. Anderson by eating a hearty meal, they sat on the front terrace awaiting Tim's return. By the time the limousine emerged from the forest, Cara had told Jessica all the reasons he had been spending weekends in the City. She omitted nothing, even elaborating on the relationship between Barbra and the prime minister.

"It's okay, I've told Jessica everything," said Cara as Tim approached.

Sitting down opposite them, he put his feet on a low wicker table. He leaned back, folding his hands across his chest, and sighed deeply. "I'm beat. These feet have done a lot of walking."

"But what has the head found out?" asked Jessica anxiously.

"I've got bad news and worse news," he said, trying to lighten the tension. "I visited at least a dozen government health agencies and six or seven hospitals. No one has ever heard of Barbra Weissman."

Cara was crestfallen. She had thought it would be so easy to find her. With the increasing sophistication of computers, it was practically impossible for anyone to disappear in an area as small as New York. Was it possible, she wondered, that Barbra had been transferred to some other state? If so, she was beyond their reach.

"And what did you find out about my Scarpetti test? Is a false negative test result possible or could there have been an error?" Sitting on the edge of her chair, comforted by Cara's hand resting affectionately on her forearm, Jessica waited patiently for his response.

"That's the worst news," he said as he reached over and patted her comfortingly on the shoulder. "When I was looking for Barbra, I stopped at the Scarpetti Center, the agency responsible for the testing program and the maintenance of records related to the program. I didn't find Barbra, but I did get answers to some of your questions. Within three weeks after birth, each infant's blood sample is sent to three different medical laboratories operated by the center. The results must concur. In the event there is any discrepancy, the child is immediately retested. The results must be identical before a determination of gene negative—"

Cara's heart sank as she watched Jessica's stoic expression begin to crumble. "What if the results never concur? What if, let's say, two remain positive and one, negative?" she interrupted.

Standing up, shrugging his shoulders in helplessness, he continued. "They say that in the millions or billions of tests they've done, that's never happened. If one lab's results are different on the first go-round, it's because of faulty equipment or tainted blood. On a repeat, they've always obtained identical results. And," he looked at Jessica sadly, "the test is one hundred percent reliable."

"God," she moaned, putting her head in her hands, "who am I? I feel like an alien. What's wrong with me?"

"Tim, there's one more possibility." Soothingly, she began rubbing Jessica's neck. "Did you see her test records? Maybe Jessica's records got lost in the shuffle . . . accidentally, or even deliberately. Maybe she tested positive, but got buried in the computer's negative file."

"Is that possible?" asked Jessica, feeling a sense of hope once again.

Sitting back down, he rested his chin on his hand in posed thought. "Maybe. I suppose anything is possible." He looked at Cara. "In answer to your question, no, I did not see the actual records. Only stipulated-by-name personnel are permitted access to the computers. Visitors can't get beyond the reception room. And it's well guarded."

"We can't get in there," said Cara, jumping up after several minutes had passed, "but I bet Barbra Weissman can get computer access."

"What good is that if we can't find her?" they asked, almost in unison.

"It means we have to find her," she said simply, as though their successful search was now assured. "Tim, how about that reporter, Sherry Ryan? Suppose I put her on Barbra's trail. I'm sure she can be trusted and reporters are good at this kind of thing. Heaven knows they're always able to find out more about me than I want them to." Feebly, unsure of the strength of her conviction, she looked at Jessica.

"Why don't we begin with a good night's rest? It's been a long day for all of us, and there's some practicing I have to do before I go to sleep." Looking at her with adoration, she winked suggestively at Cara, and the two of them walked into the house, leaving Tim sputtering to himself about what a good idea it was to talk to Sherry Ryan.

Twenty-Three

Waiting for Sherry outside the press room, Cara's thoughts were interrupted by a bemused Angelico who stood up from behind his desk and joined her at the door. "Ms. Romero," he bowed slightly, "good morning. It's a pleasure to see you again. Is everything to your satisfaction? Are there any problems?" Reaching up, he straightened his tie, slicked back his hair, and waited for her response. "Of course," he asserted when she didn't immediately answer, "this office will do anything it can to be of assistance to you."

"You can relax, Mr. Angelico, this has nothing to do with you." Turning her back to him, she continued to watch the elevator doors.

"Oh," he said, obviously disappointed. With her back still toward him, he leered lustfully at her behind before reentering the office.

"Sherry, how about that lunch?" she called out as the pudgy reporter appeared. "I'm sorry I didn't get back to you sooner, but the conference has been keeping me busy."

"Well, yes, that would be fine," said Sherry, eyes wide, surprised that Cara was waiting for her. "When you didn't respond to my notes, I thought I might have to visit Cali for our luncheon. What day is good for you? Any day but Wednes—"

"How about today?"

"Today?" repeated Sherry, confused by the sudden attention. "Well, uh, let me just check my schedule to be sure I can clear things." Pulling out an appointment computer from her back pocket, she scanned it, while Cara hovered over her shoulder, trying to think of all the things she could say in the event that she tried to put her off. "Great! I can rearrange a few things." Talking more to herself than to Cara, she pressed a few buttons, and smiled at the Calian who appeared to grow more attractive each day. "No problem. How about meeting me in

doi:10.1300/5559_24

the press dining room right off the main restaurant? No one uses it on a Monday, so we can get some privacy there."

The morning conference session passed agonizingly slowly and it was the first time that Cara could not stay focused on the agenda. Her mind kept slipping to thoughts of Barbra. The need to find her was so much greater now than it was when she left Cali . . . for wholly selfish reasons.

Arriving in the press dining room at 12:00 sharp, Sherry Ryan immediately grabbed a corner booth where it was less likely that their conversation would be overheard by other patrons. She wasn't sure why Cara finally agreed to meet with her, but she did know that she wanted the meeting to be conducted in total privacy. Sherry had her own secrets to share. Restlessly waiting for Cara, she read and reread the menu, realized that she hadn't comprehended a thing, and tried reading it again. "Damn," she muttered in exasperation as she slammed the menu on the table, "maybe I should just send her a letter." She was about to get up to see if Cara was waiting in the hall when she saw her enter through the adjoining restaurant.

"I'm sorry. The morning session broke later than usual and I just got out, but we have an extra half hour for lunch and if you have no other plans, we can extend our luncheon." After Sherry nodded in agreement, she continued. "Let me just make a quick stop in the ladies' room and I'll be right back." As she rushed off, Sherry found herself trying to define the word charisma.

They chatted politely as they both ate salads, discussing their work backgrounds, the success of the conference, and Sherry's recent rise in prominence as a reporter—the direct result of Cara's kindness in granting her special admission to the briefing. Thirty minutes later, tiring of the chatter, Sherry nervously pushed the plate away and methodically refolded her napkin, waiting to see if Cara would begin the conversation.

"I'm not going to beat around the bush on this," Cara finally began. "I need your help." Immediately, Sherry took out her press computer, put it in the middle of the table, and pushed the switch to audio. "No," exclaimed Cara as she reached across and moved it back to the off position. "This is not on the record. I need your promise of full confidentiality before I speak."

"You've got it," responded Sherry, relaxing a little bit when she realized that there would be an exchange of secrets.

"There is someone in this country whom I urgently need to find. Tim Felmar has been looking for her since our arrival, with no success. It was our understanding that she was in New York City, but now we're not sure."

Leaning forward, Sherry's face suddenly became a mask of seriousness, her fingertips tapping on the table. "Go ahead, Ms. Romero. Continue."

Cara heard herself take a deep breath, suddenly not quite sure that asking for a reporter's help was the right thing to do. "She's a physician, about sixty years old, a documented lesb—"

"And in 2018, she had a daughter named Cheryl."

Not quite sure of what she was hearing, Cara cocked her head to one side, a look of incomprehension spreading across her face.

"My maiden name, Ms. Romero, is Cheryl Weissman. My mother's first name is Barbra. Barbra Weissman is my mother," she said, slowly and distinctly, smiling slightly as she saw Cara's expression change to one of understanding.

"But . . . how . . . how did this happen? It's just too coincidental." Leaning forward with her elbows on the table, she shook her head in consternation.

"Hell, it's no coincidence. I've been waiting to meet you for the last six weeks. I badgered my office to get this assignment. You got me into the press briefing, but I got myself assigned to your visit. I had no idea you were looking for my mother. I just knew that I needed to talk to you."

"That's incredible!" mumbled Cara, not used to being at a loss for words. "What did you need to talk to me about?"

"I want you to help me get my mother to Cali." Once said, Sherry breathed a sigh of relief, feeling the doubts of commitment fading.

"Do you think she wants to go to Cali?" Whispering now that more people were coming into the dining room, they moved their heads closer together.

Sherry shrugged her shoulders. "Hell, remember me? I'm the unopinionated woman reporter." She smiled weakly. "I don't know. Actually, we've never discussed it. I know she loves Miriam Ekstrom. And I'm a big girl now. It's about time she gave me up." There was a long pause while she disdainfully wiped away the tears that were starting to form. "Damn, I'm such a wimp."

"Where is your mother now? In Cali, there's a rumor that she was transferred to New York City three months ago. But Tim Felmar has queried almost every government agency, researched all computer records, and even checked with other gays, and we haven't been able to find a trace of her."

"Your rumor was one hundred percent correct. Without warning, Mom was reassigned from the *Fantasia* to Scoge, an obscure agency in New York that provides specialized care for children of government employees. The Olms, followers of the hate doctrine preached by that bastard Olmstead, got word of a lesbian's presence and picketed Scoge." Her pudgy face reddened in anger and she reached for her glass of water. "My mother's patients and co-workers were furious with the Olms, but they couldn't make them stop. Mom, already depressed about leaving Miriam Ekstrom for a second time, threw in the towel and decided to call it quits. She retired four weeks ago." She took a long swallow of water and solidly placed her empty glass on the table.

"When can I meet with her?" asked Cara, her heart beating so fast, she wondered if she would live long enough.

"Wednesday, Mom will be coming to my house for dinner. That would be a perfect time. It'll be just the two of us. My husband—he's also a journalist—is in Europe on assignment for the next month. You can join my mother and me for coffee." Now fully relaxed, Sherry smiled the smile that Cara had found so spectacular when they first met.

"It's good to see that happy expression again," she stated with a wink. "Wednesday is fine. Write down the address and plan on my arrival after nine o'clock." Hesitatingly, she looked at the clock and began gathering her things, preparing to leave. *No,* she thought. *I've got to give her warning.* "Sherry, I won't be coming alone. There's a woman I met in New York who will be with me." She watched Sherry's expression change to bewilderment. "I will be glad to help your mother, but I also need to ask her to do something for me. I need to have your mother access Scarpetti gene records to determine whether this woman tested positive or negative in 2026."

"Hell," said Sherry scratching her head in thought, "she must be negative or she would have been shipped to Cali by her third birthday."

Leaning over the table to block out any possibility of being overheard, Cara spoke softly. "I'm not sure. This woman and I have become lovers." She hesitated for what seemed forever. "Her name is Jessica Mooran," she finally divulged.

"Holy shit!" was all Sherry said.

Twenty-Four

—◈◈◈—

"My father is the president of the United States. I've met queens and kings and emperors," said Jessica as she kept shifting her weight and rubbing her hands nervously in the limousine, "but I don't remember ever being this hyper."

"Relax, my love." Cara smiled, trying to convey a confidence she wasn't sure she felt. "Just keep in mind what Tim said. This woman is on our side. She is a lesbian. She is also the lover of the prime minister of Cali."

"I think that's what's making me nervous. Your prime minister scares me."

"Miriam Ekstrom? She's wonderful. A big teddy bear. Think of her as a lesbian Golda Meir."

"Who is Golda Meir?" asked a bewildered Jessica as she teasingly threatened to start biting her fingernails.

"Just a lady from Milwaukee." Cara smiled, pressing the button to cut off the video to the driver's section. "As soon as we get to Cali, you, dear heart, are going to get an intensive lesson in women's history." Grabbing her hands, she kissed the tips of each of her fingers.

Smiling reassuringly to Jessica, she rang the bell to Sherry Ryan's house at precisely 9:00 p.m.

"Ms. Romero, Ms. Mooran, it's a pleasure to welcome you to my home," said Sherry, hands trembling as she opened the door. "Please come with me." They followed her into the small living room, where Cara, who had become increasingly fond of the American reporter, warmly hugged her. "Please call me Cara outside of the formality of the conference center."

"And I'm Jessica." Reaching out to shake her hand, she thought better of it and grabbed Sherry in a quick hug instead.

doi:10.1300/5559_25

"I can't believe it. One day I'm standing outside the Southwind Hotel and a few days later, I'm being hugged by the daughter of the president of the United States. Life really is a blast."

"I'm Barbra Weissman," interrupted a slight woman who entered the living room through a side door. A measurable silence permeated the air as Cara stepped back to study Miriam Ekstrom's lover. Barbra, much tinier than she had anticipated, surprised Cara with her delicate, almost fragile appearance. She and her biological daughter had little in common. Barbra was petite, the glasses perched on her nose almost too large for the small oval face which bore more wrinkles than could be explained by time alone. The years had not graced her well. Heavy eyelids covering light brown eyes saddened her, while graying hair portrayed a pale, faded impression. But there was a dignity about the woman, an elegance that conveyed good manners and quality breeding, and when she spoke, the melodious voice rang with a seductive quality. *This is a woman people listen to,* thought Cara.

Without hesitation, Barbra assumed leadership of the meeting as she warmly shook hands with the two women. "I'm pleased to meet you both, of course, but I'm especially pleased to meet a co-worker of Miriam's," she smiled, surprising Cara with an early acknowledgment of her relationship with the prime minister. "I know why you have come to visit. My daughter told me about your luncheon. Why don't we get to know one another and enjoy some coffee or tea and dessert before we begin our discussions." Nervously, her fingers rubbed a pin that was affixed to the collar of her pale gray business suit. When she moved her hand, Jessica saw the engraved initials "M.E."

Following her lead, Jessica and Cara helped themselves to the beverages and finger cakes brought in by Sherry, and conversed casually with their hostesses about ordinary things.

Putting her cup back down on the table and removing her napkin from her lap, Barbra signaled that she was ready for the more serious issues. "I understand," she said, looking at Cara, "that one of your missions, assigned to you by Sherry, is to aid me in emigrating to Cali. The question, of course, is not whether I would be allowed into Cali, but whether I wish to go." She smiled politely at her listeners. "I know I will disappoint you, but I cannot answer that question at this time.

There are many things I have to consider before I make that decision. I have to consider that going to Cali may mean that I will never see Sherry again." She reached over and affectionately squeezed her daughter's hand. "I also have to consider how my immigration would affect the life of Miriam Ekstrom."

In the pause that followed, Cara began to speak, "The prime min—"

"I'm not asking you for an answer, Cara," interrupted Barbra. "Nor am I asking a question to which you could possibly know the correct response. Only one person can determine how my immigration would affect Miriam Ekstrom, and that person, of course, is Miriam Ekstrom. Now, if you want to help me—"

Unhesitatingly, Cara nodded.

"Then this is what I would like for you to do. During your break in Cali, before your final week in New York, I would like you to ask your prime minister a question. Ask her if there are slippers in the closet."

Cara, expecting Barbra to continue, suddenly realized that she was waiting for her to speak. "I'm not sure I understand. Let me make absolutely certain that I'm hearing you right. You want me to ask Ms. Ekstrom, 'are there slippers in the closet?'"

"Yes," answered Barbra patiently, "just like that. She will understand the question. And if she doesn't understand, then that will be my answer."

When she grasped that there would be no further explanations, Cara pressed the record button on her watch and with a sheepish, shy smile, said aloud, "Are there slippers in the closet?"

"Good," said Barbra, clapping her hands to indicate that she was finished with that topic. "Now, what can I do to help you?"

In detail, Cara and Jessica described their relationship, Jessica's desire to go to Cali, and the problem concerning the Scarpetti gene. "And so that's it," summarized Cara. "We have been told that there could have been no error on the test, which leaves us with the possibility of Jessica's records being improperly categorized at the Scarpetti Center as gene negative."

"That's a remote possibility, but it is a possibility," agreed Barbra.

"Mom, you can access the computer's files, can't you?" asked Sherry, her voice squeaking in urgency.

"Relax, dear," she chided her daughter. "Yes. Because of my work on the *Fantasia*, I am one of the stipulated-by-name persons who can access Scarpetti files." Smiling broadly, Jessica turned to Cara, and quickly kissed her on the cheek.

"I'm sure my name has not yet been removed from the list," Barbra continued. "Elimination or addition generally takes about six months. However, I think it would be wise if I did not attend to the matter before Sunday. There are too many people present on other days who may remember that I no longer work for the government. Yes, I think Sunday would be most favorable."

Walking over and hugging the surprised Barbra, who felt even tinier to Cara as she leaned over and wrapped her arms around her, she tried not to sound too hopeful. "Thank you, Dr. Weissman. Thank you for trying on our behalf."

"You're very welcome. But please keep in mind that all I can do is access the records and review them. If the records state that Jessica is Scarpetti-gene negative, there is nothing that I can do to alter them."

"Yes, we both understand," volunteered Jessica sadly.

For the next hour, the four women spoke as old friends. Cara, enjoying the unique opportunity to share with a group of American women, joined in the laughter as she described her diverse experiences in New York. "Seeing a female prostitute was quite a shock, but seeing my first pregnant female was even more astonishing. I couldn't imagine what was wrong with this woman and so there I stood in the conference center elevator just staring at her. After a few seconds passed, she asked me if I wanted to feel the baby kick, and I looked around the elevator, trying to find the baby. I was red-faced for the next several days over that one."

"Don't Calian women ever become pregnant? Do they always adopt? How about artificial insemination?" asked Sherry.

"My dear Sherry, no respectable Calian woman would chance having a baby that would turn out to be heterosexual and have to be deported," said Barbra. "And there's a good chance that's what would happen. After all, you were the product of artificial insemination . . . a very gay man and a very gay woman. Unless there's something you're not telling me, we produced a very heterosexual baby."

After the laughter died, Barbra, who had been chortling as heartily as any of them, became serious again. "Cara, I want you to know how very proud I am of you and Tim Felmar. I've been following the extensive publicity you have received, and you have both made a very fine impression upon the parents of Cali's babies." She reached into a pocket and, removing a tissue, gently dabbed at her eyes. "Surrendering a child is one of life's most painful experiences. I felt its touch thirty-five years ago, when I thought of giving up my own infant. And I saw it every day on the docks of the *Fantasia*." She sighed deeply, her mind reliving the chaotic scenes of screaming women proclaiming their agony. "To the mothers who live with that pain, you and Mr. Felmar represent their lost children. You have given them hope that the lives of their offspring will be better than their own. Your countrymen and countrywomen should be very pleased with what you have accomplished here."

Cara squirmed in her chair, appreciating the words, yet uncomfortable with her role as heroine to a society from which she had been discarded. "Thank you for the kind words, Dr. Weissman. The Americans have been very gracious to me, but I still don't understand why—if they recognize themselves as our family—why do they allow the Olms to continue to persecute gays and lesbians?"

"Because we wimps are afraid of them," responded Sherry. "The bastards hold this country hostage through fear, intimidation, and the invocation of the name of God. They preach insane and screwed-up doctrines of hatred and violence, and we listen."

"All that is changing, dear," exclaimed Barbra, placing her hand lightly on her daughter's arm to restrain her from further eruptions. "Since that horrible beating of Brian Rayford, the gentleman from your country, the Olms have dwindled in number and power. When there are too few left to capitalize on the fears of the weakest among us, America will embrace all of her children."

"Dr. Weissman, are you saying that the day will come when the United States will stop banishing homosexuals?" asked Jessica, not quite sure that Cara wanted to hear the answer.

"Yes. Yes, I certainly am. And you, my dear," she asked, turning to Cara, "what do you think about that possibility? What do you think Cali will do if America stops exiling its homosexuals to your island?"

"We will do the same thing that we would do in the event that the United States reestablished abortion to eliminate the Scarpetti gene. We would institute a genetic alteration program that would enable the women of Cali to produce homosexual children. And, naturally, we would continue to accept voluntary Scarpetti-positive immigrants."

"So, there will always be a Cali," smiled Barbra.

"Yes!" exclaimed Cara with unmistakable passion.

"Such lovely people," proclaimed Barbra after Cara and Jessica took their leave, Barbra promising to let them know the results of her Scarpetti Center visit by Monday. "Now dear," she announced, turning to her daughter with her hands clasped in front of her in schoolmarm fashion, "you and I need to have a serious talk about our future."

"How did I know that was coming?" sighed Sherry.

Twenty-Five

The four days till Monday passed with the lumbering grace of a turtle.

"How can it be that you leave in less than nine days and each minute seems like an hour?" asked Jessica as they sat in the entertainment room on Friday night. "I would expect it to seem as though time is flying."

"And for sure, that's the way it will seem once we get past Monday. So, my love, let's not rush these minutes. I want to enjoy them to the fullest."

"And we will, because I have a surprise for you," announced Jessica, biting her lower lip mischievously, her eyes grinning with excitement.

"You are my surprise," responded Cara, reaching over and brushing the soft black hair with her fingertips.

"No. This is a real surprise!" she said emphatically as she crossed the room to the cabinet opposite and returned with a pile of what appeared to be flat cardboard packages. Pulling out a black, circular disc, she explained, "This is called a record. There's one in each of these cardboard holders, known as jackets. There's music on here that can be played on a phonograph machine. They were actually made between 1960 and 1985."

Cara looked at her quizzically.

"That's the way they recorded music in those days . . . on phonograph records. I remembered them when you were at the conference today and I rummaged through the Hargreaves collection—most of it is stored on the second floor—until I found them. And," she smiled seductively, "I even found the phonograph machine. If you are real nice to me, I might play some romantic records for you."

© 2006 by The Haworth Press, Inc. All rights reserved.
doi:10.1300/5559_26

"How nice is real nice?" asked Cara, trying to conceal her aroused grin.

"Nice enough to join me for a midnight swim . . . in the nude."

"Why you little imp!" she laughed, pulling Jessica down on the couch and covering her face with kisses. "You would trade anything for a swim in the nude."

"Sunday night? A date on the beach?" Her left eyebrow rose flirtatiously.

"Deal!"

Again checking the switches on the control table to make sure that the entrances to the entertainment room were locked with a dead bolt, Jessica wrapped herself around Cara and kissed her longingly. "I lived twenty-nine years without ever comprehending the meaning of lust. And now it totally consumes me."

Tenderly, they made love to the sounds of k. d. lang, Barbra Streisand, Dinah Washington, and others whose songs were obliterated by their increasing passion.

"I have to leave for DC tomorrow morning," Jessica said as they lay quietly on the couch, the voice of Patsy Cline filling the room. Seeing the disappointment on Cara's face, she quickly added, "I didn't want to upset you before we made love."

"Why?"

"Why didn't I want to upset you before we made love?" teased Jessica, trying to prolong their contented mood.

"No," she responded, jabbing her gently with an elbow. "You know what I mean. Why do you have to go to DC?"

"My father returned from his Asian tour on Wednesday. Tomorrow night he's hosting the annual diplomatic reception. It's an event in which I've participated as his hostess. I can't say no to him."

"Jessica, you know that once you go to Cali, you will probably never see your father again." Somberly, she turned her head so that she was looking directly into the muted gray eyes. "Is this a problem we need to discuss further?" *Maybe,* Cara thought uneasily, *this is where the search for truth ends.*

"Oh, Cara, I know what you must be thinking. But, that's not it. I haven't seen him for four weeks and I don't know how to say no to him without having to explain things. Until we know something definite, there's no reason for me to upset him. Please trust me," she said with a sincerity that could not be questioned.

"When will you be returning?"

"Sunday evening . . . in plenty of time for our midnight swim."

"I didn't think you'd miss that," she said, trying to smile.

Twenty-Six

Jody waited for the phone to ring four times before she finally turned it on. She had just walked into the kitchen to put breakfast in the cookery when it began its insistent wail. Margo was still asleep, and she had no interest in exchanging telephone pleasantries on a Saturday morning when the day off gave her the opportunity to return to bed and cuddle with Margo while their meal was being prepared.

"Wait a minute," she responded when she recognized Cara's voice. "Before you say anything, let me check the line for clearance." After a brief pause, she came back on the receiver. "No good. The audio is bugged. Hang in. . . . Ah hah," she exclaimed proudly a few seconds later, "the video is cleared. No problem. We'll sign."

Cara related her success in finding Barbra and their subsequent meeting at Sherry's house, carefully omitting any mention of Jessica.

Jody, visibly excited, signed, "What do you think? Will she come to Cali?"

"I don't know. Sherry wants her to go, so I don't think that will be an issue. Apparently, it's going to depend on how the prime minister answers a question Barbra instructed me to ask."

"What's the question?" asked Jody.

Feeling foolish, she vacillated before responding.

"Well?" signed Jody. "You know I won't repeat anything we've discussed to anyone except Margo, who has more of a need to know than either of us. I'll treat it as priority one."

Feeling herself blush, Cara wondered how good the color reception was on Jody's monitor. "'Are there slippers in the closet?'" she signed, encountering some difficulty remembering the symbol for slippers.

"Hang on, Cara. I think we're getting some interference. Something is disturbing your transmission. Let me check the lines again."

doi:10.1300/5559_27

She returned a few seconds later. "No problem. We're not being bugged. Repeat your last signing."

After several frustrating repetitions, Jody signed back, her face screwed up in exasperation. "I can swear you said 'Are there slippers in the closet?' Are you sure that's what you meant to sign?"

Now giggling, barely able to move, Cara excused herself and breathed deeply until she was sure she had regained control. "Yes," she managed to nod.

The two women laughed uproariously, tears rolling from Jody's eyes as she commented, "I'm glad you're the one who will be asking that question and not me." There was a brief pause before she was able to stop chuckling and change the conversation. "Before we terminate this transmission, I have a message for you from Vanessa. She asked me to tell you that she and Anisette are now at war. Your bossy cat didn't like her new woman friend, so on Wednesday she jumped on Vanessa's back and began howling every time they started making love. She finally put Anisette outside the door, but she kept right on howling. Vanessa said it was the worst night of her life."

"Every night that she can't make love is the worst night of Vanessa's life," laughed Cara.

"You know something," signed Jody, sitting at her kitchen table, running her fingers through her yet uncombed hair, "It's good to hear your laugh again. That's the part of you I had missed the most."

"I bet that's not what Vanessa says about her old lovers," she teased affectionately, "but thank you for that. I needed to hear some kind words."

"Oh?" queried Jody, always sensitive to Cara's moods. "I've read all your press. Has something been omitted?" Shouting to Margo that she was on a long-distance call, she again signed to the monitor, "Cara, is there anything you want to tell me?"

Cara hesitated, wishing she could alleviate some of the tension by sharing Jessica with Jody. Her legal mind and nurturing temperament could be invaluable, but the story was too complex to relate over the telephone, particularly with their rusty signing skills. "Just one thing. Please call my mothers and tell them I'm well, happy, and very safe. Anything else I have to tell you will wait until my return."

"When do you get back?" she asked, her face frowning with concern.

"Friday night, but I probably won't speak to you until the beginning of the week. I'll need a few days to put myself together."

"Good, let's talk. Lunch or dinner as soon as you're able."

Switching off the transmission, Jody removed the breakfast tray from the machine and brought it into the bedroom, setting it on the table next to Margo. "Something is wrong with Cara," she announced as she kissed her on the forehead.

"Any idea what it can be?"

"No, she was very cautious. Too cautious. She looked a little too tired and her words were a little too constrained. At first I thought it was related to our signing, but I think it was more than that."

"What about Barbra? Any progress there?" asked Margo, as she swallowed a spoonful of poached eggs. "Mmmmmm. Cooked to perfection."

"Barbra is another story. I think we would like this woman very much," she said as she again began laughing.

Twenty-Seven

On Saturday afternoon, Cara insisted that Tim escort her to an antique shop, her curiosity piqued by the Hargreaves phonograph.

"What do you want to go there for?" moaned a reluctant Tim.

"Because it's raining. Because there's nothing else to do. Because we don't have antique shops in Cali. And because I'll go crazy if we sit around here all day," she said, standing in the dining room, gesturing theatrically with her hands.

"Ms. Romero is right," said Mrs. Anderson as she walked in and began clearing the luncheon plates. "There are several little antique stores on University Street. You know where that is, eh? And they have the most wonderful things on display. You'll see, Mr. Felmar. You'll have a grand time. It's sort of like exploring the past."

Mrs. Anderson was right. They had a wonderful afternoon discovering things they had never heard of before. There was a telephone that once had to be cranked before speaking into a mouthpiece affixed to a square box that hung crookedly on the wall, a hand-operated grinder for coffee beans, and an efficient little electrical machine that was used for opening something called cans. Cara had heard about cans, but saw her first one when the shopkeeper demonstrated how the machine opened the rigid round aluminum container that released sweet smells of chocolate syrup.

"You were absolutely correct," Tim told the housekeeper when she brought in the evening dinner of chicken pot pie and salad. "Those shops were something else. They were more like museums than Cali's museums."

"See? I knew you would have a good time," stated the round-faced woman proudly as she put their plates down before them. "Mrs. Anderson wouldn't tell you wrong, eh?"

doi:10.1300/5559_28

Tim ate with his customary, hearty appetite, chiding Cara who picked at her meal, her hunger abated by the sight of the empty seat across the table. She pushed the food around on her plate, hoping that the good-natured housekeeper would not be offended by the amount left uneaten.

"Why, Ms. Romero, you've hardly touched a thing. I suppose you're lonely without Miss Jessica here, eh? But she'll be back tomorrow." Acting as if she had said nothing of importance, Mrs. Anderson nonchalantly carried the plates into the kitchen.

"I can't believe she said that," said Tim, mystified. Cara simply shrugged.

After he left to go to the entertainment room and Mrs. Anderson retired for the evening, Cara washed the dishes and then retreated to her bedroom where she turned on the White House station and dialed for all the events of the day. Hours later, barely able to stay awake, she became instantly alert when her attention was caught by Jessica standing next to her father. She was wearing the pale pink dress that they had selected in the Stony Brook boutique, and now, with her soft ringlets framing her face and her copper skin glowing tanner, she looked even more alluring in it than Cara had remembered. Briefly, the camera moved to other scenes, and then, seconds later, videos of the actual dinner reception appeared on the monitor. Cara's face contorted in shock as she saw Jessica chatting happily with the young man who had brought her home a few days ago. Her fiancé, Roland.

Twenty-Eight

—◦≪≫◦—

"I'm going to lose her before I even have her," Cara said to Tim late the next morning. "I've never felt this kind of jealousy before. Competing with a woman is one thing, but I don't know the first thing about competing with a man. The worst part is that I don't even know the rules of the game. Does she or does she not have the Scarpetti gene?" Pressing the button on her watch, she reviewed her vital signs. "I'm so angry, I'm surprised I'm still alive," she snickered, as she swam to the other side of the pool.

Trailing after her, Tim grabbed her by the wrist. "Relax, Cara. Whatever you saw, I don't think it meant anything. I'm as sure that Jessica loves you as I am that Glen loves me."

"What makes you so sure of Jessica?" she asked, breathing deeply, trying to exhaust her anger as she swam back to the other side.

"You've got to stop swimming back and forth if you want me to talk to you," he yelled across the pool. "I'm not a very good swimmer and I'm about to have a heart attack."

"Okay," she said, jumping out of the pool and throwing herself onto a chaise lounge.

"Thank you." He bowed as he scrambled out and took a seat beside her. "Now you're going to have to give me a few minutes to catch my breath before we continue this conversation."

"I'm scared, Tim. I've always been so sure of my intuition, but this time, maybe it's wrong. Maybe she is just curious about lesbians. Maybe I'm staking all my hopes on a genetic impossibility."

"Cara, don't do this incredible woman a disservice by insulting her character. With or without the Scarpetti gene, she's not playing a game. She loves you, but she's scared too." He paused to see if she was listening. "In the next few weeks, one of two things will happen to

doi:10.1300/5559_29

Jessica, and they're both a losing situation. If she emigrates to Cali, she'll lose her family and the prestigious life she's known for the past twenty-nine years. If she's not allowed to emigrate to Cali, she'll lose you. She's under tremendous strain, so if she spends a night with friends and manages to forget her problems for just a few minutes, don't be angry at her. I'm sure she'd still rather be here with you."

Sitting up, Cara put her elbows on her knees, covering her face with her hands. She sat for a few minutes, absorbing the silence so saturated with thought. "You're right," she declared, pushing her wet hair back from her forehead. "You're absolutely right."

Several hours later, they were just finishing dinner when Jessica came running into the house. Hugging Mrs. Anderson first, she then ran around the table and simultaneously grabbed Tim and Cara. "Oh, I've missed you so much," she whispered in her ear.

At midnight, they walked down to the beach, stopping just long enough for Jessica to dismiss the security men and request that the two women be transferred to their guard for the rest of the night, and then they continued on to the Lair.

"You've told me all about your conversation with Jody and your visit to the antique shop, but you haven't asked me about my trip."

"I knew you would tell me when you were ready," she answered as she spread out the blanket, weighing down the edges with their towels.

Sitting down, curling her feet under her, Jessica leaned over and kissed Cara sweetly on the cheek.

"Uh-uh, that's not part of the deal. This is a nude swim only. No kisses. No hugs. No sex."

"But Cara," she said, lower lip pouting childlike, "it's dark. No one can see us. Making love to you on the beach is my favorite fantasy. I can just envision you with your blonde hair melting into the sand and the water lapping at your feet and your fingers digging into the ground. . . . Aren't I tempting you just a little bit?" Trying not to smile, she turned her head to the water, peeking at Cara sideways, only the uncontrolled lift of her left eyebrow revealing the light-hearted play of jesting.

"You are a tease, Jessica Mooran," she exclaimed, shaking her finger in mock anger. "But," she smiled, "when we get to Cali, I'll get even. Now, tell me about your trip."

"My father looked wonderful. His trip to Asia was successful and he had lots of good stories to tell. The dinner reception was okay, but it would have been more fun if you had been there. I could have made eyes at you across the table."

"Wasn't there anyone else there you could have made eyes at?" asked Cara, annoyed at herself for surrendering to baseless doubts.

"As a matter of fact, there was," she volunteered. "The White House protocol officer didn't know that I had broken my engagement—I wanted to tell Dad first— so Roland was assigned as my escort. Seeing him only made me miss you more," she said lovingly as she stretched out on her stomach, hands at her sides.

Cara leaned over and barely brushed her lips against Jessica's back.

"I thought you said no kisses," she yelped, surprised at how quickly her body always responded to Cara.

"That's right, but that little freckle just needed to be kissed," she said, her heart filling in spots she never knew had emptied. Leaping to her feet, she bent over and pulled Jessica up by the hand. "Come on. It's time we went for a swim."

Laughing, they raced down the beach into the cold water, each woman grateful that the evening had not been spoiled by the mention of Barbra and the visit she had made earlier that day to the Scarpetti Center.

Twenty-Nine

As she got off the elevator, Cara spotted Sherry waiting for her by the auditorium door. She started to walk faster, but stopped when she realized that the flat expression on Sherry's face did not convey the answer they had fervently hoped for.

"I'm sorry," she said as Cara came closer. "The records show that Jessica Mooran tested negative. Mom checked all the laboratory results. They're identical."

"Oh, my God." A sickening feeling spread through her body. "How do I tell Jessica?"

"Do you want to go for some coffee?" asked Sherry, her eyes reflecting her share of the pain.

"No. I'm okay. Please tell Tim Felmar. He's probably in the entertainment room next to the press office." Comfortingly, she clasped Sherry to her chest, speaking in a barely audible voice. "This is not going to end here. I'm not going to allow that bastard Olmstead and laws borne of hatred and ignorance to win. Jessica and I are going to grow old together. Somehow, I'm going to get to the bottom of this."

"In my unopinionated way," commented Sherry, heavy with the knowledge that she was watching her mother grow old alone, "I think you should go for it."

The rest of the day was a waste. Trying to block her mind of Jessica proved fruitless. Her biggest concern now was how to tell her, how to keep her focused on the future, free of the insidious distrust forged by despair.

Returning to the estate early in order to be there before Jessica arrived from her first day back to work, Cara sat with Tim on the terrace, trying to clear her mind of the pain. *I need to free my brain in order to think,* she told herself, running her fingers through her hair.

doi:10.1300/5559_30

"If you keep doing that, all those beautiful tresses are going to fall out. Now, let's try to solve this problem together. What's the next step?"

"How do you know there's going to be a next step?"

"Because I know you, Cara, and I know you're not going to let it end here," he said, folding his arms across his chest and leaning back, balancing his chair precariously on the hind two legs. "You're just like your predecessor. Miri Mills never let anything stop her. And I'm betting you won't either."

"Right on all counts," she said as she began to use her hands for gesturing.

They sat and spoke for almost an hour before Cara, knowing that Jessica would be returning any minute, left him on the terrace, asking that he extend apologies to Mrs. Anderson if they didn't appear for dinner.

"You want me to tell that sweet woman that you're going to miss a Monday night special? Besides, who's going to do the dishes?"

"Better get your towel ready, my man," she said, in better humor than when they had first returned from the conference. Supported by the encouragement of Tim, she mounted the stairs with a lessened sense of foreboding.

She washed her face, changed to more comfortable clothes, and was ready a few minutes later when Jessica pushed open the bedroom door, her face shining with the excitement of expectation. "What's happening? What did Barbra find out?" she asked, crossing the room to sit on the bed next to Cara. She looked at her face and back down at the floor. "It's not good, is it?"

"No," she answered. "The records were correctly categorized. The lab tests were negative. But——"

Leaping from the bed, Jessica raced down the hall to her own room. Slamming the door to the bathroom in front of Cara, she had barely locked it before her face beaded into a cold sticky sweat. Dropping to her knees, she hung her head over the toilet, vomiting repeatedly until all that was left were the spittles of bile that drooled bitterly from her mouth. She pressed her face against the cold bowl and sobbed in a voice not unlike the women who had lost their children on the docks of the *Fantasia.*

In the irony of the bedroom that had been Ellyn Hargreaves's, Cara slumped to the floor, listening to the cries that tore at her innards. When she finally heard the spigot turning and water hitting the basin, she knew that the worst was over.

Pulling Jessica to her as soon as the door opened, she held her tightly, kissing her forehead with fervent tenderness. "I'm not giving up, Jessica. You are going to be in Cali with me. I promise you that. Now," she said as she kissed each of her eyes, "let's move on to the next step."

"What's that?" asked Jessica, reaching for the tissues that sat on the night side table.

"I'll tell you outside where we can watch the sunset as we talk."

Sitting on the wrought iron settee, her feet perched on the railing of the balcony, Cara spoke earnestly to Jessica who sat beside her. "You know I love you." She didn't wait for an answer. "There are some questions I need to ask that may be disturbing. I will love you no matter what the answer." She took her hand and tenderly kissed each finger.

Confused, Jessica nodded with hesitance.

"Is it possible that you tested Scarpetti-gene positive and your father bribed someone to alter your records?"

"I had already thought about that," she responded without being defensive. "And the answer is definitely no."

"Why are you so adamant?" she asked, her hopes dwindling.

"My parents would have to have done that before I was three years old, and twenty-six years ago they could not have afforded to bribe anyone. My father was a school administrator, my mother was a receptionist in a doctor's office. They didn't have the money."

"How is that possible? What about Mrs. Anderson? How could they have afforded a housekeeper?"

"They couldn't. Mrs. Anderson had been their neighbor. My parents took her in several years before I was born, right after her husband left. She worked as their housekeeper in exchange for room and board. Later, when Dad changed jobs and began earning more

money, they paid her a small salary. It's been that way ever since."
Jessica's eyes again began to fill.

Ignoring the blossoming tears, Cara pummeled away at Jessica's family. Was there anyone they knew at the Scarpetti Center who would have altered the records as a favor? Were there any relatives who might have been involved? Did Mrs. Anderson know anybody? Where did Mrs. Anderson's husband work?

"No! No! No!" screamed Jessica, finishing the conversation. "This is going to get us nowhere. The records were not altered. The truth of the matter is that Jessica Mooran tested negative."

"Well then, we're just going to have to test you again," announced Cara, jumping up and slamming her hand on the railing.

"How can you do that?" asked Jessica, suddenly hopeful again.

"I don't know yet, but you can be damn sure I'll find out. I can't ask questions in this country without arousing suspicions, but I can ask in Cali. Jody is an attorney. In the ten days that I'll be there, she'll have enough time to get us some answers."

Disappearing into the bedroom, Cara returned with a light afghan and draped it around Jessica's shoulders to ward off the cold evening air. Sitting down beside her, she held her hand as they were slowly engulfed in the descending darkness, no sunset visible in the heavily overcast sky.

Thirty

There was almost nothing Cara could do to alleviate Jessica's suffering during the next two days. "I need to know what I am and who I am," she explained each time Cara tried to comfort her. "How can I love you as much as I do? What's happening to me?"

"Jessica, there's nothing wrong with you. Something is terribly wrong with your Scarpetti records, and I promise I'll find out what it is. Please trust me."

"I'm trying," she said with a heavy heart.

On Wednesday evening, she felt a little more upbeat when they again visited Barbra and Sherry.

"I've made half of my decision about going to Cali," said Barbra, after they had finished the formalities of coffee and cake. "Sherry, why don't you tell our guests what you have told me?"

"I told Mom that I could no longer allow her to remain in the United States because of me. I love her very much," she paused and smiled proudly at Barbra, "but I no longer need a mother to take care of me. At this point, Ms. Ekstrom needs her more than I do, and Mom needs Ms. Ekstrom more than she needs me. They should have the opportunity to grow old together." She winked at Cara. "Mom was worried that she would never see me again if she went to Cali, but," she reached over and picked up a newspaper that was laying on the coffee table, "just as soon as she leaves, I'm going to start using this weapon to make sure that some changes are made in the relationship between our two countries. You can bet your sweet ass that I'm planning to see my mother again."

"Bravo. Well done," said Cara as she reached across and shook Sherry's hand.

doi:10.1300/5559_31

"So, my dears, that leaves the decision in the hands—or the slippers, to be more precise—of Miriam Ekstrom." She reached over to Jessica, taking her hands in her own. "And you, dear girl, you know, of course, that if I go to Cali, I will use whatever influence I can to make sure that you come right behind me. Do not fret. I will do my share to persuade the powers that be. I can be very persuasive, you know." She put her hand over her mouth and chuckled in feigned embarrassment.

Later that night, Cara and Jessica made love for the first time since Sunday.

Thirty-One

Thursday was a bittersweet day.

It was the final day of the World Conference on Aging and also the day before Cara was to leave for Cali for the ten-day break until the legislative follow-up to the conference.

As they wrapped up the final hours, the conferees voted to honor Cali's first Director of the Office for the Aging by establishing the Miri Mills Trophy to be presented annually to the conference participant who had made the most significant contribution to the field of aging during the preceding year. Although the first trophy would not be presented until 2056, it was generally acknowledged that Miri's successor, Cara Romero, would have won the award for 2055. For Cara, it was enough to know that the efforts of Miri and the accomplishments of Cali were being recognized.

Celebrating over lunch with the European homosexuals who had presented the proposal for the Miri Mills Trophy, Cara nonchalantly asked, "What is life like for gays and lesbians in your homeland?"

"I've seen great changes," said Liza, the eighty-five-year-old from Denmark, "but it's nothing like Cali. I visited your country several years ago. It is much more free than anything we Danes even dream about. If I were younger, I would emigrate there. Then I wouldn't have to worry when I wink at the young women on the streets."

"Or when you chase them," chuckled one of the Swedish men.

"In Sweden," began the man called Lars, "we enjoy great freedoms, but we are still treated badly by some of the majority. Occasionally, there is still, what they call uh . . . uh . . ." The young man pulled out his computer translator and labored over it for a few seconds. "Fag bashing," he said, looking at his companion who was still laughing with Liza. "It is not always safe for us on the streets, especially when people have been drinking during holidays. Sven and I argue sometimes about taking risks. He is not always careful."

As the Europeans ate their meals, Cara lapsed into thoughts about something Barbra had said. "Now, dear, I had thought of moving to Sweden so that my loved ones from Cali and the United States could both visit me. Sweden does not discriminate, of course, against Calian passports, which meant the door was open for my Miriam as well as my Sherry. I decided against it, however. It seemed like an awfully complicated way to solve one's problems by arranging it so that you don't live near either of those you love." *But,* thought Cara, *what if Jessica and I both moved to one of the Scandinavian countries?* Not desirable, but possible.

When the afternoon session ended early and Tim was not waiting for her in his usual spot, Cara went down to the press office where she found him speaking with Michael Angelico.

"Oh, here comes our girl now," she heard him say as the two men looked in her direction.

"Ms. Romero, I'm honored that you chose to visit this office on your final conference day," said Angelico as he shook her hand. Clearing his throat, he tugged at his shirt collar and straightened his perfectly knotted tie. "I want you to know that it has been a pleasure to be of service to you. And to Mr. Felmar too, of course," he added as he looked at Tim. "You have both made a very good impression upon the Americans. Leona—my sister who sent her son to Cali twelve years ago—watched every one of your television interviews. She is a different woman since you arrived."

"Why, thank you, Mr. Angelico. Those are very nice compliments. On behalf of Tim and myself, I want to thank you for all your hard work and for the wonderful living arrangements you set up for us."

They spoke for a few more minutes, Tim advising Angelico that he would be calling him with their flight plans for the one week legislative follow-up. The men agreed that the arrival information would be classified confidential to preclude any future problems at the airport.

"I don't think you have to worry about the Olms anymore, Ms Romero," he said as they were about to leave. "In view of your popularity, I am sure they will not do anything to disrupt your visits to this country. When you return, do you think you would prefer to stay at a residential site closer to the conference center? I would be happy to make those arrangements for you."

"No, no, certainly not," she said quickly. "The current arrangements are perfect. I'm much happier being near the water. It keeps me from feeling homesick." Looking directly at her, Tim raised his eyebrows in amusement.

During the limousine trip back to the estate, Cara tried to maintain an upbeat attitude, sharing her thoughts about Europe with Tim.

Tim grimaced in displeasure. "Well, it's a possibility that wouldn't make me very happy. I've gotten used to spending time with you and I wouldn't want to have to go to Denmark to do it. Have you thought about living separately in Cali and the United States and vacationing in Europe together?"

"No," she said quickly. "That's not an acceptable solution for us. Barbra and Sherry Ryan are considering it as a possible way to visit with each other, but Jessica and I need to do more than visit. She is going to live in Cali with me," she said, slapping her hand on her knee as she turned away to look out the window.

After dinner, Jessica led her to the entertainment room. "I have something for you," she said after she checked the console to make sure they were in total privacy. Reaching into her pocket, she pulled out a small box topped with a bright red ribbon.

"That's exquisite," said Cara as she removed a small heart-shaped gold locket, delicately engraved with flowers. "I've never seen anything like this. It's beautiful. I absolutely love it!"

"It's an antique." Reaching over, she took it from Cara's hands and opened it to reveal a tiny black ringlet of hair and a photo of herself. "This kind of locket dates from the 1900s. It's the sort of gift people gave to one another to symbolize the memories they carried in their hearts." With her hands, she cupped Cara's face. "I want you to always carry me in yours."

"Always," said Cara, as she kissed the brimming tears and pulled her close.

Thirty-Two

—◦∾§∾◦—

"Well, you sure don't look good to me," argued Sue as she scrutinized Cara on her home office monitor.

"I'm fine, Mom. Really, I am. I got off the plane less than an hour ago and the trip was exhausting. But I'm feeling wonderful, so you can stop worrying." Scooting Anisette off her lap, she stood up and walked to the window.

"Don't expect me to stop worrying until you come back from that last week in New York."

"By the way, Mom, did you ever hear of a gay bar in the city called Stonehenge?"

"No. Not that I recall. Stonewall maybe, but not Stonehenge. Uh-oh, there goes my office phone. It's probably Tom Feldman. Only Tom gives someone less than two minutes to answer." She switched the incoming call to the hold position. "You know, next year, I think I'm going to start commuting again. This home office plan just isn't working. I spend more time on the phone than on the computer."

"Well, why don't you take Feldman's call? There really is nothing else for me to report. Give Donna a big hug and kiss for me. I'll call again later in the week." Turning off the telephone, she stared at the deep blues of the Pacific and tried not to think about Long Island Sound.

After unpacking her suitcases and putting away the glasses Vanessa had left in the dishwasher, she turned on the phone and called Jody.

"I didn't expect to hear from you until Monday or Tuesday," she said as Cara's face appeared on the monitor. "Should I tell you how tired you look or would you prefer that I not mention it?"

doi:10.1300/5559_33

"Sue already told me. It's not something I need to hear twice. Look, before we go on to pleasantries, please check your calendar to see if we can schedule dinner for tomorrow night."

"I don't need to check. I already know. Saturday night won't work. We're going to Bob and Paul's commitment ceremony."

"Oh," said Cara, a little offended when she realized that she had not been invited. "How about tonight?"

"Tonight?" repeated Jody, her face reflecting her surprise. "I thought you didn't want to see me for a couple of days. Yeah. Sure. Tonight's fine. Just let me check with Margo. I'll call you back if we need to re-schedule. Cara, are you okay? You're acting very peculiar." She watched her face, looking for some kind of reaction.

"I'm really fine," she said, running her fingers through her hair.

"No, you're not. I know that gesture all too well. Look, why don't we forget Topanga's. Too many people recognize you there. There's a new Italian restaurant called Dante on State Road Seven, right off Park Boulevard. The food's good and we'll be able to get some privacy."

"Sounds good to me. How about seven thirty?"

"You got it. See you then," said Jody, switching the phone over to "locate" so she could clear it with Margo.

By 7:15, Cara was already seated in a booth sipping a cold glass of Rochambeau Chardonnay. Over and over she rehearsed in her head how she would present the issue of Jessica. She needed to present the problem in a way that would enlist Jody's aid in sorting through the bureaucratic legal maze in which Scarpetti-gene testing was mired. That meant presenting it in an organized, analytical fashion. With Jody, two and two always had to equal four and shades of gray were nonexistent.

"I can't believe you got here before me," said Jody as she leaned over and kissed Cara before taking her seat on the opposite side of the booth. "You must really be in trouble for that to happen."

"Not in trouble. In love." Cara took an exaggerated swallow of wine and awaited Jody's reaction, which was not long in coming.

"Wait a minute. Did I hear you right? Was there another Calian escort besides Jim or Tim or whatever his name was?"

"The attorney I've known and loved would say 'meal first, business later.' Is that still the rule?" she asked as the waiter interrupted with the menus.

"Even I make exceptions in special cases. And this is a special case."

Cara related the story, omitting few details, while they slowly ate their spaghetti with clam sauce. Jody interrupted several times, trying to pin down the specifics of locations and dates. "Jody," Cara finally yelled with uncharacteristic exasperation, "this is not a case of mugging or fraud. It's a love story that revolves around a goddamned gene."

"Okay," said Jody when Cara had finished a few minutes later. "Now it's my turn." Drumming her fingers on the table, she sighed deeply. "Oy, where do I begin?"

"Begin with what you know. Tell me about the law."

"Cara, as you said, this is not a case of mugging or fraud, and I am more than your lawyer—I'm your ex-lover. I'm also your friend. You're going to have to give me a few minutes to digest this and spit it back out." *So beautiful and so determined,* Jody thought as she watched Cara signal the waiter and order two glasses of Kahlúa, Cara forgetting that Jody never drank after dinner. Jody began talking again after the drinks were delivered. "Cara, as your ex-lover, friend, and lawyer, I must say this: there is no Cali in Jessica's future and no future for you with Jessica. Whether you love her or she loves you, it doesn't matter. There's no diplomatic relationship between our two countries. Neither is going to bend on this issue, especially when we are dealing with the daughter of the president of the United—"

"Dear heart," Cara interrupted, reaching across and taking Jody's hand, "I am not going to bend on this either. Giving up Jessica is not one of my options. Nor is it an issue for discussion. So, if that's where you're heading, you can stop right now. All I'm asking is whether it's possible to have Jessica retested for the Scarpetti gene in either Cali or the United States?"

"Damn! You are so bullheaded," Jody said, squeezing Cara's hand warmly before releasing it to take a swallow of the Kahlúa she hadn't intended to drink. "Then we have to move on to the lawyer-only stage. In answer to part one of your question, it's not possible for

Jessica to be tested in Cali for the Scarpetti gene. Our laws are quite clear and not subject to misinterpretation. Legislation passed in the early 2020s allows us to test for the gene under two circumstances only. We can retest Calians and new émigrés whose positive results are subject to question. We can also test children under the age of six, a measure to prevent Calians from trying to raise their own Scarpetti-negative biological children. In other words, we're only allowed to test those whose *positive* results may be in error or children under six years old. Legally, Jessica does not meet either of those requirements. She's negative and well past six."

Cara listened intently, not interrupting or commenting, reacting only once when she nodded her understanding of the much-publicized "biologicals ban" law that created the program of random testing for children under the age of six. Fingering the floral engraved locket that hung from a chain around her neck, she asked with urgency, "What about part two of my question? Is there any way that Jessica can be tested a second time in the United States?"

"No. Many years ago, the United States passed a law preventing any citizen from being tested more than once for the Scarpetti gene. The law was promulgated to prevent the harassment of effeminate persons or others thought to be homosexual by the followers of Olmstead. Prior to its passage, the Olms overloaded laboratories by insisting that some people be tested eight or nine times. A suit brought before the Supreme Court resulted in the passage of the first American law that actually struck a blow against their power."

"Can we challenge that law?"

"That would be tough. It's a sacred American law, one that Cali very strongly supported. It could take months or years of legal haggling."

"Even if the law was challenged on the basis of the fact that the test is being requested by the individual to be tested?"

"Yes. There are no exceptions to the law. That's one of the virtues of its passage. It assured that the Olms could not physically force an individual to request a second test." She swallowed the rest of her drink and looked at her watch, surprised that it was only 9:30. "Your best bet, Cara, is to see if the prime minister will intercede for you and assist you and Jessica by making the request part of the considerations for strengthening diplomatic relations between the two countries."

Cara, who had been trying to sop up the spaghetti sauce she had spilled on her shirt with a stain-remover wipe, shook her head. "That's not going to happen. We both know Ekstrom. She isn't going to put Cali in the position of being turned down by the United States on an issue regarding homosexuality. I can't ask that of her."

"What then? Relocate to Europe? I sure as hell wouldn't want to see you exercise that option."

"Well, then start preparing your lawsuit. You said it would take months or years of legal haggling, so I suggest you get started in the morning."

Putting her hand on Cara's shoulder, Jody almost regressed to the stuttering of her childhood. "You're . . . you're . . . you're kidding me, aren't you?"

"Hell, no. I'm angry," said Cara, gesturing so adamantly she almost knocked down the tray of coffees carried by a passing waiter. "Somehow, Jessica was documented as being Scarpetti-gene negative by the United States. My heart, my head, and this locket tell me she's positive. And I'm asking you to challenge the American laws that keep us from retesting her."

"Damn, you're stubborn," said Jody, taking a long swallow from Cara's glass of Kahlúa.

Thirty-Three

—◦≪⨾≫◦—

"So, how's my favorite secretary?" asked Cara as she bounced up to Esther's desk on Monday, dramatically removing two gift-wrapped packages from her briefcase and placing them on top of the mound of papers and discs in the in-box.

"Oh," exclaimed Esther, standing up and racing around to hug her boss, "I didn't expect you quite this early. I thought you might even take the day off." Stepping back, she looked her up and down as though trying to determine whether the New York trip had changed her appearance. "You look wonderful. A little tired, maybe. Your skin is so tanned. You must have been spending a lot of time in the sun. Is that possible?"

"Of course. Even conferees get weekends off. Now, I want you to open your gifts."

"Three pounds! I might even share it with Marge," she joked as she unwrapped the oversized box of New Jersey saltwater taffy that Cara had mystifyingly bought in New York. "How did you know that it's my very favorite candy? And it's more than thirty years since I've tasted any."

"I knew because you reminded me every day for the two weeks before I left." Teasingly, Cara put down her briefcase and changed her smile to a scowl, placing her hands on her hips in a reprimanding posture. "I was afraid to come back without it. Now, the next package. That's the one that was my choice."

"I'm going to save this paper," announced Esther as she carefully folded the wrapping paper stamped with old-fashioned photographs of the Empire State Building. "Oh, my," she said, sitting down and leafing through the stack of picture post cards that Cara had carefully

doi:10.1300/5559_34

selected for her at the Stony Brook antique shop, "this is wonderful. Oh, the memories."

"If it's so wonderful, why are you crying?" asked Cara as she picked up her briefcase and walked into her own office. Esther jumped off her seat and followed behind. "Now, it's time to go to work before you embarrass me with more tears. What's been happening here?"

"Not very much. We've all been so busy following your adventures in New York. I'm very proud of you, Cara. You've accomplished so much. That first press briefing, your speech, and the Miri Mills award. I knew you deserved that assignment." Sitting down opposite Cara, she pulled a tissue from the desktop box and removed her glasses to wipe her moistening eyes. "Just look at me. I'm becoming a sentimental old fool."

"Hey," yelled Cara, "I won't have you talking about my favorite secretary that way." Giving Esther a chance to regain her composure, she quickly turned on the computer and reviewed the messages. "You're right. Not much has been happening here. I do have lots of work for you, however." Opening her briefcase, she pulled out a small box no bigger than a deck of cards and handed it to her. "Here's all the computer audios from the conference. The last few squares contain my reviews and impressions. I audioed daily when traveling back and forth to the conference center and made my final summations on the plane trip back. I'll need a hard copy —it'll be several hundred pages probably—by this afternoon. Think you can get it done by the time I return from lunch?"

Esther counted the number of shiny squares. "Of course. I'll probably have it before you leave. The audio-copier spits out more than one hundred pages an hour. Now, just to remind you, there are two critical messages on your computer. One is from the PM's office requesting a Wednesday meeting. I responded in the positive. The second is from Tim Felmar who said he arranged for a very early flight to New York on Saturday. He said that you had some important things to get back to." She paused and looked at Cara with raised eyebrows. "Weren't you supposed to fly out on Sunday?"

Cara grinned broadly. "Uh-huh."

After Esther left the office shaking her head in confusion, Cara softly whispered, "yes!" and clapped her hands, then began rummaging through the written notes that had collected during her three-week absence. Burrowing into her computer, she occupied her mind with the work of the Office for the Aging, clearing her head of genes and conferences.

At 12:30, Esther brought in the hard copy of the computer audios. "I did a little listening while these were being transcribed. Your voice bubbled with enthusiasm. It sounded like you really enjoyed that conference."

It wasn't that conference, it was that woman, thought Cara as Esther handed her the documents and left the office. Separating the papers into neat piles on her desk, she began to leaf through them, and decided instead to bring them home to study. Her ability to concentrate had atrophied in a scant three hours.

Leaving the office early, she stopped at Fausto's for some groceries, stocking up on cookery packages before arriving home. Trying to balance the packages and her briefcase while unlocking the door with her keycard, Cara very nearly tripped over Anisette, who began winding around her ankles as soon as she gained entrance. "You're a killer cat," she muttered. "You're lucky Jessica likes kitties or I'd give you to Vanessa." The cat meowed loudly and ran under the couch. "Only kidding, Anisette." Purring, she crawled back out, belly low to the ground, looked around, and again began rubbing against Cara's legs.

Lying on the bed with Anisette attached to her side, she tried to review the conference reports, her concentration continuously interrupted by visions of Jessica. *This will never do,* she thought, as she got up and took a leisurely shower, feeling very alone without the sound of Jessica's playful giggles.

After a quick dinner, barely eaten, she dialed Vanessa, who clicked in almost immediately.

"Cara, is that you?" she asked, standing naked in the kitchen, a towel in her hands. "Holy shit, you caught me just out of a shower. I was sure it was Louise. Oh well, you may as well see what I'm offering all these wonderful women," she said as she laid the towel over a chair. Strutting back and forth in front of the peach-colored refrigerator, her arms at her sides, she stuck out her tongue at the monitor, and disappeared from view.

"That wasn't bad," assessed Cara when Vanessa returned wrapped in an oversized purple robe, her wet frizzy red hair now piled on her head under a turban. "I must admit, however, that's the first time I ever saw red pubes."

"If you're lucky, maybe I'll let you see them again one day." Hearing Vanessa's voice, Anisette's ears perked up. Leaping from her favorite chair, she cautiously crawled low to the monitor and swiped at it with her paw. "You miserable critter. After all I've done for you," said Vanessa, hands on hips.

"It must have something to do with your carrot top. Maybe she doesn't like redheads."

"I don't care what she likes. It's her mistress I care about," said Vanessa with a teasing wink. "Look baby doll, why don't I throw on some clothes and stop by for a visit. I'll bring back your keycard in case you want to pass it to some other broad for the rest of this week."

Running to the door as soon as she heard the bell, Anisette lovingly rubbed up against Vanessa's legs as soon as she entered the living room. "What can I tell you? Schizophrenic cat," Vanessa shrugged as she plopped onto the couch next to Cara, Anisette curling up in her lap.

Cara adored Vanessa. With the red frizzy hair she referred to as "barely kempt" and the spreading freckles that matched, she lived up to her fun-loving guise, but it was her good-hearted disposition that Cara found most endearing. She was a marshmallow in the hands of women . . . and there had been a lot of women who liked marshmallows.

Vanessa leaned over and kissed Cara on the cheek. "I know you're too busy to take the time to make love. So why don't you just tell me about your trip instead?"

In less than an hour, she described her experiences in New York, Vanessa oohing and aahing in all the right places. Only once did she bedevil Cara. "I don't get it. There you were with the opportunity to avail yourself of a female prostitute, and you turned it down. What kind of a lesbian are you? Three weeks without sex—she would've paid you for that performance."

When she finished describing her trip, carefully omitting any references to Jessica, she reached into her pocket, brought out a small box, and put it on the table in front of Vanessa. "And as a special thank you for taking care of her while I was gone, and allowing her to snuggle with your dates, this is from Miss Puss," she said as she petted Anisette, who was purring contentedly in Vanessa's lap.

"Miss Puss has excellent taste," proclaimed Vanessa after opening the box and removing a pair of silver earrings. "They're spectacular. I've never seen such good filigree work, and in my fifteen years as a silversmith I've seen a lot of good stuff. These must be antiques—1900s quality." Hugging Cara in a viselike grip, she planted a wet kiss on her cheek. "Baby doll, if you keep treating me like this, I'll be yours forever." Squeezed between the two women, Anisette snarled loudly, jumping to the floor on silent feet. "Don't worry Anisette, forever is only until next week." Looking again at Cara, she asked "Speaking of. . . . What is our schedule for next week? When do you leave?"

"Before we talk about that, there's a favor I need to ask of you."

"Anything for a celebrity." Unceremoniously, she picked Anisette up from the floor and plopped her back in her lap.

"I want you to design a silver identification bracelet in the shape of a heart. On the front, I want you to engrave 'Jessica,' and on the back, 'Cara.' Under 'Cara,' put the date 'January 1, 2056.'"

"Hey, this sounds like serious stuff. Do I know this chick?"

"No, but you will. If this incredible woman accepts, January 1 will be the date of our commitment ceremony. You'll be invited, of course." Her face displayed no absence of conviction. *I have to believe,* she thought. *Whether it's here or in Europe, we will celebrate the new year together.*

"No shit!" Vanessa lowered her voice to a conspiratorial tone. "Does anyone else know about this? Mary Jane or Kate? How about Toni?"

"For now, you're it. I'm counting on you to keep it that way."

"You've got it. You've also got my promise of the most beautiful bracelet ever designed, baby doll, but are you sure you don't want it in the shape of a cat?" she asked as she cradled a squirming Anisette.

Thirty-Four

Standing in the vestibule outside the prime minister's office, Cara tugged on her green pin-striped jacket, sat down, stood up, paced back and forth, and sat down again. Repeatedly, she pressed the play button on her watch and listened, "Are there slippers in the closet?" *Will I really have the courage to pose that question to the prime minister of Cali?* she asked herself, feeling the heat rising in her cheeks at just the thought.

Jonathan, the PM's receptionist, who was accustomed to the discomfort of visitors, merely smiled and continued working at his desk as though nothing unusual was occurring. Finally, when a bell rang he spoke to her. "Ms. Ekstrom will see you now. You can go right in."

With a gesture of self-assurance, she assertively pushed open the massive plastic doors and walked up to the prime minister, who was standing in front of her desk. Extending her right hand in greeting, she was surprised to find herself suddenly swallowed up in Miriam Ekstrom's powerful bear hug.

"I am kvelling," said the PM, holding her at arms' length, yet close enough for Cara to feel the heat of her breath. "That's an old Yiddish word from my American ancestors. It does not translate well. It means that I am more than proud. I am filled . . . no, I am overflowing with pride. Now," she said, releasing Cara and returning to her seat behind her desk, "please sit down and tell me all your thoughts about the country of my youth. The media reports have told me about your successes, but they have not told me about your impressions. You must tell me that yourself."

Cara spoke freely, describing the dirty streets of New York, the odors wafting up from the subways, the vandalized churches wrapped with graffiti, and the prostitutes lining the streets. "I saw much that

doi:10.1300/5559_35

was bad, but I also saw much that was good," she said as she went on to describe her experiences with the media, the security personnel, and the citizenry. "The Olms were never a threat. They're a dying breed who are out of favor with the American people. Despite any efforts of the Olms, I was treated very warmly by everyone I met, even the stuffy three-piece-suited diplomats." She suddenly stopped and looked apologetically at Ms. Ekstrom.

"It's okay, Cara. Most diplomats are stuffy. We have a few ourselves. Tell me more about the Miri Mills award. Was it opposed by the United States representatives?" She leaned forward at her desk and peered at her with great intensity. Cara didn't know why, but the answer was obviously important.

"No, to the contrary. The award was strongly supported by the Americans. It was their lobbying that pushed it through," she answered, restlessly moving about in her seat as this phase of the conversation appeared to be ending.

"Sit still, Cara. We're not finished yet," she admonished, as she stood and walked to the window, leaving her anxiously pondering what was to come next. "During the past six months, President Mooran has been quietly campaigning for the establishment of better diplomatic relations between our two countries. He wants Cali and the United States to open the borders to mutual tourism. He wants to lift telephone and mail restrictions. The fact that the Miri Mills award received the approval of the American public and the success of your visit has made the president even more steadfast in his determination. He is very pleased with the effects you have had upon his constituency, and so am I." She looked at Cara with a warmth rarely seen by subordinates.

Responding with a hesitant nod, Cara silently speculated about the president's reactions to the effects she was having on his only daughter. Her tongue felt heavy in the apprehensive dryness of her mouth. "I'm very flattered," she managed to say.

"So now you see why I am kvelling. This is the first time that the superpower has come to us in an effort to normalize relations. It's an important step forward for our tiny country, Cara," she smiled, "and I am sure the next phase of your trip will take us even further." Standing up, she indicated with her silence that the interview was at an end.

Cara stood, but didn't move. Several times she opened her mouth, but looking directly at the prime minister, she couldn't seem to say the words she had so carefully rehearsed.

"What is it?" asked the PM. "Is there something you want to say to me?" When she realized that something was amiss, she walked over to Cara, lightly resting her hand on the younger woman's shoulder. "What is it? Just spit it out, Cara."

Gathering her courage, she ignored her reddening cheeks and looked directly at Ekstrom. "Are there slippers in the closet?"

"What—" the PM began to say, abruptly stopping herself. Raising her eyebrows, she glared at Cara in consternation, the glow of recognition suddenly flashing in the dark eyes. For the next few moments, the two women motionlessly stared at each other, exchanging a barrage of unspoken questions. "Yes," she said, returning to the seat behind her desk. Still, Cara didn't move. "That will be all. You may go now, Cara." The prime minister picked up her pen with a visible tremor and began reviewing the daily assignment sheet, her eyes softer than Cara had ever seen them.

Thirty-Five

⌒◦≶◦⌒

Unable to concentrate on her legislative briefings in the VIP lounge, Cara decided to move up to the body of the plane and sit with Tim.

"I can't seem to get the wag out of my tongue this morning," she said as she sat down and poked him in the ribs with what Jessica's night voice described as her bony elbow. "Come on Tim, wake up and speak to me. It's six thirty a.m. and we're going to be landing in less than an hour."

"We spoke for almost two hours on the telephone yesterday. I'm out of speak. Besides, I'm a night person. I shouldn't be awake at this hour," he mumbled, turning his back to her and pushing his head further into the pillow.

"If you talk to me, I'll show you the bracelet."

"That's insufficient enticement. You already told me all about it."

"Well then, I'll—"

"You told me about the PM too. So, forget that. How about telling me that you're going to get a little shut-eye for the next half hour?"

"Are you grouchy this morning or is it my imagination?" she asked, realizing that the teasing was a bit more caustic than usual for her good-natured traveling companion.

"I'm grouchy every morning, as the angelic Glen would tell you." Sarcasm saturated the word "angelic."

"Oh?"

"Nothing major. A small domestic. He's not happy about me being out of town so much. I just didn't think he should pick four a.m. to register his protests." He pressed the button, converting the recliner back into a seat, and looked out the window, watching the morning sun reflecting off the inverted-V wings. "He is right, though," he said,

doi:10.1300/5559_36

shrugging his shoulders as he turned toward her. "If we're going to adopt a baby, I need to spend more time at home. Being on the road half the year is not a great plan for raising a kid."

"Well, why don't we just add that to our list of problems to solve?" she asked, lifting her hands, palms up, in question.

"I think your plate is already full." He laughed. "Glen and I will be all right. I just need to be a little fairer. I really can be a tyrant at home."

"You know, I always thought that about you," she said, tongue in cheek.

"Why, you stinker!" he exclaimed, his eyes grinning before his mouth got the message.

They were amicably chatting, his spirits raised a bit, when the plane landed at MacArthur Airport at 9:15, New York time. The flight had been uneventful and they were able to deplane without incident. "I guess we're yesterday's news." Cara smiled. "If we ever come to New York again, maybe we'll even be able to wear Calian clothes. Disdainfully, she put on the frumpy American jacket. "Whoever heard of combining black and gray stripes? I wonder what Calvin would say about this?"

As they walked away from the conveyor belt, a pasty-faced elderly man came rushing toward them. Instinctively, Tim dropped the valises and stepped in front of Cara. Sizing him up, Tim knew that he could overpower the man with ease, but remained standing in a defensive posture.

"Ms. Romero," said the man as he pushed a pen and paper at her, "please, may we have your autograph? Me, and Jenny here," he grabbed the hand of the woman who stepped up behind him, "we were just standing, waiting for our son's plane to come in. Jenny—she saw you first."

"I knew it was you, right away," said his wife. "But you know something, you're even prettier in person. We don't mean to bother you or anything."

"That's perfectly all right," said Cara, signing her autograph as Tim remained vigilant. A small group began to gather, and she signed several more before Tim signaled that it was time to leave.

"Why did you stop me? I was enjoying my celebrity status," she said as they rushed toward the waiting limousine. Suddenly, he stopped walking, threw down the luggage, and roughly grabbed her wrist to keep her from going any further.

"That's not Lenny," he said insistently, staring at the driver holding open the door.

"No, it's not," she said as she watched the involuntary rise of the slender driver's left eyebrow touching the black ringlets that were falling from under the cap. "She's in drag," Cara yelped as she ran forward and embraced the amused Jessica.

"These people," said Tim, nodding at the crowd that had gathered at the airport window, "are going to think Calians are crazy." Kissing Jessica on the cheek, he pushed her into the backseat with Cara and took the position behind the driver's wheel. "What will tomorrow's newspapers say?"

"How did you manage this?" asked Cara as she helped Jessica take off the driver's uniform jacket and removed the cap from her head, while planting small kisses on any piece of exposed flesh that passed her lips.

"This one was easy," she said as she pressed the button for solid window tinting and longingly embraced her. "I've missed you more than I ever thought possible," she whispered. Still clinging tightly to Cara's hand, she explained. "This was a cooperative effort. I told Mrs. Anderson what I wanted to do and she arranged it with Lenny. I think she was tired of seeing me mope around the house."

Arriving back at the house, Tim and Cara went directly to the dining room where Mrs. Anderson was preparing breakfast. She pulled them both to her overly endowed breasts, smacking a wet kiss on each of their cheeks. "Welcome back. We're all so glad to see you, eh?" Nodding in Jessica's direction, she added, "Some of us more than others."

It was early afternoon before Cara and Jessica were finally able to walk to the Lair, the cool September weather keeping them from changing to bathing suits. "I like it so much more when I can see the fibers of your flesh," said Cara as they sat down on the grassy area. Looking at Jessica, she noticed, with sadness, that her bright glow of summer was dimming, the copper tan fading like the hours of sunlight.

She told Jessica about the prime minister's startled reaction to the question about slippers in the closet and then, sitting with shoulders caved, stared wistfully at the rippling waters of the Long Island Sound. "I spoke with Jody," she finally said. It was a conversation she had been avoiding since her arrival.

"Shhhhhhhh," said Jessica, kissing her finger and putting it to Cara's lips. "It's all right. I already know. While you were gone, I had lunch with Doris. She's been a friend since college, one of the country's best international attorneys . . . works on my father's staff. She gave me the answers I didn't want to hear."

"Those answers are not final, Jessica. Jody is preparing the briefs to challenge the laws. And we are going to win. We are going to be together in 2056, even if it means going to Europe to live until the case gets to court."

"Cara, honey, that would never work. You belong in Cali. You are Cali. You would never be happy in Europe. I couldn't allow our relationship to be swallowed up in the bitterness that would ensue," she responded adamantly, her voice lending conviction to the words.

"I'm not going to give you up—"

Again, Jessica put her finger to Cara's lips. "Shhhhhh. Let's not talk about this now. We have a wonderful eight days ahead of us. Let's enjoy one another and share in Barbra's happiness." She moved her face closer to Cara's, removing her finger and placing her full mouth against hers.

I am kvelling, thought Cara. *I am filled to overflowing with this woman.* "I have a surprise for you," said Cara, breaking the despondent mood.

"You know how I love surprises." Jessica clapped. "What is it?"

"First, I remove your watch from your left wrist," she said as she took off her wristwatch and put it in her back pocket.

"I like this game," said Jessica, eyebrow raised flirtatiously.

"Next," said Cara, "I kiss your eyes closed." Lightly, she brushed Jessica's eyelids with her lips. "Then, I kiss each of your tiny fingers." Picking up her left hand, she seductively suckled the tip of each finger, moving from one to the other by weaving her tongue along the sensitive flesh of the palm.

"I can't stand it," said Jessica, starting to giggle as she tried pulling her hand back. Playfully, Cara held on to Jessica's squirming wrist as the two women wrestled affectionately on the grass. Suddenly, Cara stopped, her face masked in confusion as she forcibly gripped Jessica's forearm. "You're hurting me," yelled Jessica. "What's wrong?"

Staring at Jessica's wrist, her face paling in shock, Cara's eyes focused on the white strip of skin that had been hidden by the watch. "That's not a tan line. You haven't been in the sun for weeks," she said aloud, more to herself than to Jessica. "What is this?" she said, pointing to the two-inch long rectangular patch of white skin.

"It's a scar," she responded. "I don't know how it got there. I've always had it."

Grabbing Jessica by the hand, Cara ran, half dragging her, back to the cliffside stairs. Panting, more from fright than exhaustion, Jessica pleaded with her to stop. "What are you doing? Have you gone crazy?" she yelled, her face riveted in fear.

Two security men ran up to them, guns at the ready. "Are you all right, Ms. Mooran?" asked the one named Bob.

"She's fine," answered Cara, who continued holding her hand as she began climbing the stairs.

"It's okay," nodded Jessica, gasping for breath as she struggled to keep up.

Rushing into the main house and pushing the doors open to the kitchen, Cara ran up to Mrs. Anderson, who was standing at the stove stirring a pot of chili. "What is this?" Cara yelled, holding Jessica by the left forearm so the elderly housekeeper had a clear view of her wrist. "Why is there a laser scar on Jessica's wrist? I've seen this same scar before . . . on the bodies of Calians whose biological mothers mutilated them with messages before putting them aboard the *Fantasia*. Why was Jessica tattooed?"

Hands trembling, the old lady turned off the stove and put her wooden spoon on the counter. With great care, she took off the starched apron, hanging it on the hook of the door frame, and shuffled into the dining room, motioning for them to follow. "Why don't we sit in here where we can talk, eh? I'll tell you everything you want to know, Ms. Romero." With saddened eyes, she looked at Jessica who was shaking her head in confusion. "It's okay, Miss Jessica," she said, patting her on the shoulder. "It'll all be okay. I'm ashamed that I didn't tell you a long time ago."

They sat at the table and waited for the old housekeeper to speak.

"Jessica is not Jessica," sighed Mrs. Anderson, eyes focused on the little girl she had raised.

"I need to know exactly what's going on here," interrupted Jessica, releasing Cara's hand. "What's this talk about a tattoo? And what do you mean by I'm not Jessica? Who the hell am I?"

"I'll tell you everything, Miss Jessica. I just need time to get my thoughts in a row. You see, when you and your sister were born—"

"My sister!"

"Yes. Now you are going to have to be quiet and let me speak, Miss Jessica," she scowled, her eyebrows furrowed to the hairline. "You and your sister were born to the Moorans in 2026. Two beautiful twin girls, you were, names of Jocelyn and Jessica. We were all so happy." She smiled at the memories. "But just two weeks later, when you were tested for the Scarpetti gene, your mother's heart almost broke. Little Jocelyn—that was you—tested positive. Your sister, Jessica, tested negative. Margaret was brokenhearted when she found out that she had to send one of her beautiful babies to Cali, but she had no choice, eh? Then, when she heard that some of the Scarpetti children were being tattooed with messages, she asked Dr. Simon—that was who she worked for—to tattoo your wrist with the name 'Henry Mooran.' She thought that maybe one day you would return from Cali and be able to find your family. Eh?"

"Why was I never sent to Cali? What happened to my sister?" she asked as she gripped Cara's hand in full view of the housekeeper.

"Just one month after you were born, Jessica died of Infantile Darjee Disease. While you, my little leprechaun, stayed fat and healthy. And so, Margaret did what any loving mother would do, eh?"

"Oh, my God, she switched identifications," interjected Cara, suddenly sensitive to all the anguish that must have been suffered in the

Mooran house in 2026. "The death certificate was made out in the name of Jocelyn, the Scarpetti-gene positive child. And you, dear heart," she said, looking at Jessica, "were raised as Jessica, the Scarpetti-gene negative child."

"That's right, Ms. Romero. The only problem was the tattoo. Dr. Simon took care of that. He covered the tattoo with a laser patch so that no one would ever know."

"At least not until Cara came along. What about my sister? How come I never knew about her?" Jessica asked.

Mrs. Anderson took a deep breath before continuing. "I was the only one who ever knew that there had been twins. You see, there were no relatives. No one else who cared, eh? I was sworn to secrecy. The Moorans thought it best that no one ever be suspicious."

"My father . . . he knew," Jessica said, more a statement than a question.

"You have to understand, dear child. Your father loved his babies very much. He didn't want to lose both of them." She reached across the table and patted Jessica's hand, still held in Cara's. "He did the very best he could for you. After Margaret died, it was like he was possessed. He spent all his time working, trying to raise you right. He wanted you to go to the best schools and meet the right boys, eh? It was like if he worked hard enough, and you met enough people, you would find a nice young man to marry."

"But I found Cara."

"Yes," said Mrs. Anderson. "And a wonderful woman, she is."

"This is a lot to digest," said a limp Jessica, resting her head on Cara's shoulder, nuzzling against her neck. As an afterthought, she asked, "Mrs. Anderson, why did you decide to break your vow of secrecy?"

"I didn't. I spoke to your father first. I asked him last week when you were moping around here like a lost soul if I could be telling you the truth if you would be asking me. He said that he would be doing the same thing if you asked him." She put on the eyeglasses that she had removed when she first sat down. "Now, I'd better get back to my kitchen before Mr. Felmar comes looking for his dinner. I think you two girls need some time together, eh?" She hugged Jessica tightly, tears starting to peek from the corners of her eyes.

The two women walked out on the terrace and wordlessly sat in the lawn chairs facing the arriving sunset. Several minutes passed before Jessica finally spoke. "I love you, Cara, with all my heart and soul. It's just that there's so much for me to absorb right now. Give me a day or so to get my head together before we start planning our future."

"How wonderful to know that we have a future." She took her slender hand and pressed it to her lips, caressing the trembling fingers that conveyed the depths of Jessica's emotions. Reaching in her pocket, she took out Jessica's watch and put it back on the tiny wrist, electing to delay the surprise bracelet for a few more days. "And tomorrow, we can share in the joy of telling Barbra about her future."

Thirty-Six

⸻⸙⸻

"How wonderful, my dear," exclaimed Barbra after Jessica related the events of the day before. "So, you will be going to Cali after all."

Leaning back against the couch, her right arm relaxed around Jessica's shoulders, Cara responded. "Just one thing remains, Dr. Weissman. I spoke with Jody last night and she stated that we need verification that the records of the deceased Mooran baby are annotated gene positive. If that proves to be correct, then Jody will go through international channels to subpoena copies of Jessica's and Jocelyn's Scarpetti documents. Together with Mrs. Anderson's statement, the records should serve as sufficient proof to obtain Calian citizenship for Jessica."

"Of course. I will go to the Scarpetti Center this very week." Placing her teacup back in the saucer, she neatly folded her napkin in the demure manner that Cara had come to recognize as Barbra Weissman's.

Nodding appreciatively to her mother, Sherry extended her hand to shake Cara's and Jessica's, displaying the beautiful smile that had first attracted Cara's attention. "I'm very happy for both of you, but you must promise me that when this story can be told, I have the exclusive rights."

"You've got it!" they responded at the same time.

As the laughter faded, Barbra cleared her throat several times, surprised at the dry condition anxiety had generated. It felt as though her salivary glands had gone on strike. Taking a mouthful of tea, she self-consciously swirled it before swallowing. Then, she spoke. "I think I've kept myself in suspense quite long enough. So, now that you have solved your problems, you must help me solve mine. Cara, how did Miriam Ekstrom answer my question? Are there slippers in the closet?"

"With a forceful . . . unequivocal . . . yes!" answered Cara, hands slashing the air, punctuating the dramatic effect of the words.

Clapping her hands with evident pleasure, Barbra leaned over and kissed her daughter on the cheek. "I guess I'm going to Cali, dear."

The three young women, who had plotted earlier while Barbra was preparing tea, sat silently and stared at her. No one moved or said a word. They waited patiently, their faces a question mark.

"Well," said Barbra, "I guess I'm going to have to tell you my little secret." Trying to keep her eyelids from fluttering, a nervous characteristic of which she was only vaguely aware, she sat with her elbow on the arm of the chair, holding her hand to her forehead as she spoke. "When Miriam and I first met, it was the custom for homosexuals in love to have a commitment ceremony at the Metropolitan Community Church. It was a wedding of sorts, a meaningful union of love." She looked at Cara who nodded knowingly. "Similar to the commitments that are now accepted as legal marriages in Cali. Well, as I was saying, Miriam was always asking me to enter into a commitment with her, and I was always refusing." Standing up, she removed her apron and straightened her skirt before sitting down again to continue. "You see, my dears, life with Miriam Ekstrom was not very easy. I loved her dearly, as she did me, but she was absent so much of the time. She was constantly out marching for one cause or another—gay rights, the homeless, the people of Bosnia. I never knew when she would come home for dinner or even for the night."

"Were you living together then?" asked Sherry, her questioning face reflecting her eagerness to hear some of the details of her mother's early relationship with Miriam Ekstrom.

"Yes dear, we were. Miriam and I began living together the day after we met." Covering her mouth, she chuckled. "I wasn't always as proper as I am today. Now, where was I? Oh yes, one day when Miriam asked me for a commitment—it was the day after she was out all night planning a march on behalf of Vietnam veterans—I threw open her closet door and I yelled—she had never heard me yell before, but I yelled that time—'Miriam,' I yelled, 'do you see all those shoes in that closet? You have shoes for marching, shoes for campaigning, shoes for every imaginable purpose, but there is not one pair of slippers. On the day that you put a pair of slippers in the closet, I will make a commitment to you.' So, from that day on, whenever Miriam Ekstrom would ask for a commitment, I would ask if there were slippers in the closet. And do you know something, she was always so busy fighting for human rights, she forgot to buy those slippers." As if looking into the past, she spoke softly, her eyes clouded over, "Strangely, I loved her all the more for it."

"That's a beautiful story," said Cara, whose own eyes were becoming heavy.

Barbra passed tissues to the three young women as she wiped her own eyes, her hands still trembling from the telling. "When you get back to Cali, be sure to explain to Miriam that I will be there just as soon as I can clear up matters here."

Later, after they feasted on homemade pastries, the two women prepared to leave. While Barbra was excitedly relating her departure plans to Jessica, Sherry took Cara aside, mumbling under her breath. "What's wrong? You're not bubbling quite the way I would expect you to tonight."

Pivoting to turn her back to Jessica, she hugged Sherry to her breast, whispering softly, "I don't want your mother to worry, but there's one more stage for us to pass. Sometime this week, I will be meeting Jessica's father."

"Oh," said the cub reporter whose biggest story until this year was about the planned expansion of a local shopping mall.

Thirty-Seven

Returning from the conference center on Thursday, Tim and Cara had no doubts about who was visiting the estate. As the limousine pulled up to the security gate, two men approached the vehicle, guns drawn as they opened all the doors. Lenny, the driver, laconically reassured his passengers. "Don't worry. They're us." After everyone got out, and the car and their bodies were searched with weapons detectors, they were allowed to reenter and pass through the entrance to Ellyn Hargreaves's former estate.

"How are you feeling?" asked Tim as he saw the color drain from Cara's face.

"Like I'm about to be executed," she answered, rubbing her clammy hands together in her lap.

"Don't worry. It'll be a piece of cake. I'm going to be right next to you the entire time." She looked at him quizzically. "Well, I don't see why not. If he's going to have two or three security men present, I don't see why you can't have just one. Besides, I never met the president before."

Looking out the window, Cara gazed at the rolling blue-green flats of the old Hargreaves estate, her eyes resting on the low-flying birds who, annoyed at being disturbed as they prepared for their winter migration, cackled defiantly at the passing limousine. *Somewhere in the woods,* she thought, *are the doe and her two fawns, foraging for the remaining foliage that would get them through winter. And I too am here foraging. For the love of Jessica. How fitting that it all takes place on the estate of America's best-remembered Calian.*

Scooting in front of the security guards, Mrs. Anderson greeted them at the door. Seeing Cara's colorless face, she grabbed her hand, fidgeting with her fingers as they walked. "Now, don't be nervous,

doi:10.1300/5559_38

173

Ms. Romero. The president is a lovely man. He and Ms. Jessica are in the library. After you have put away your things, they would like for you to join them, eh?"

"What about me?" asked Tim, trailing behind.

"I'll be getting you something to eat in the dining room."

"Drats!" Drawing Cara to his chest, he kissed the top of her head. "Well, sweetie, I guess you're on your own. Don't worry. You're going to charm the pants off of him."

"That's not exactly what I had in mind," she laughed as she planted her hands on his chest and pushed him away.

"Well, I'm glad we got you your sense of humor back." He smiled.

"Let's hope I'm still laughing tomorrow."

After a quick shower, Cara dressed in the Calian outfit she had worn to her first New York press briefing. *He may as well see me in my native clothes,* she thought to herself, as she rubbed Jessica's locket, dangling handsomely in the V-neck of the body suit. Her confidence bolstered, she felt the color return to her face and the inner trembling gradually subside. Running her fingers through the carefree shock of hair that tumbled onto her forehead, she walked down the stairs to the library.

Bob, the regular security man, recognized her immediately and motioned for her to wait in the adjoining lounge while he entered the library to announce her arrival. "You look spectacular," beamed Jessica, who returned with him. Acting as though he wasn't there, she wrapped both her arms around Cara and pulled her in close, feeling the beat of her heart in rhythm with her own.

"How are you?" asked Cara, pressing her forehead against Jessica's, their lips only inches apart. "Are things okay?" The agent nonchalantly turned his back to them as she lightly kissed the tip of her nose. "Do we need to talk before I meet your father?"

"Everything is fine. Let's just go right in," she replied, taking Cara by the hand.

The library at the Marion Estate was like no other part of the house. It was an austere room, used as an office for the working vacations of presidents. The main rooms in the house, redecorated during Henry Mooran's first year in office, were light and bright with lots of wicker and rattan and shades of pale green and coral. Not so this room. Untouched since the term of Patrick Olmstead, the library reflected the personality of its first presidential occupant. The ashen rug and ponderous furniture, gathering light from a window smaller than a poster, cried for fresh air. An odor of dank decay impeded the nostrils with its mustiness while the September dampness suckled on the bones.

This room does not suit this president, thought Cara as Henry Mooran came bounding over and firmly shook her hand, his long face displaying the smile that had earned him the nickname "photo op." Standing better than 6'5" tall and tapered to his toes like the tine of a fork, he replicated the small-boned structure of his daughter. But it was not the body build that astonished Cara—it was the cleft that dissected his chin. Identical to the one that she loved to kiss, it left no doubts about Jessica's heredity.

"Let's go out on the terrace," he said after Jessica made the formal introductions. "It's considerably more pleasant than this stuffy room." Pressing the under-desk button that opened the outer door, the president ushered the women through, one on each arm.

"Come sit next to me," said Jessica, reaching for Cara's hand.

"It's all right," said the president, noticing Cara's hesitancy. "My daughter has told me everything. I would expect you to sit next to her."

"There's no place I'd be more comfortable, Mr. President," she responded, winking at Jessica as she took her hand and sat down on the settee.

"I suppose you are expecting me to provide some explanation for my behavior after Jessica's sister died. Well," he said as he sat down in the rocking chair, crossing his long legs, one over the other, "the only explanation I have is that Margaret and I loved our daughters. We couldn't bear to give them both up. It was simple to switch the twins' identities thirty years ago and claim that the gene-positive child was the one who died. Fooling the authorities was easy. Hell, I almost fooled myself." He stopped speaking and stared into the dimming light, rubbing his forehead as though trying to keep memories from emerging. "Jessica grew up like any other little girl. She had dolls and toys and boyfriends and girlfriends. When she was older, she dated and went to all the right parties. She met all the right men. Nice men, like Roland. But . . . I never saw her react to anyone the way she did to you."

"Daddy," said Jessica, her cheeks turning the color of the setting sun, "you don't have to tell everything."

The president unwound his body and walked to the edge of the terrace, waving indifferently to the security agent who sat just beyond hearing. "Well, it's true." He turned around and looked directly at Cara. "I knew Jessica was discovering herself when she first wrote to Cali on my letterhead requesting your press clippings—"

"How did you know about that?" asked Jessica, her eyes wider than that of the doe peeking from the forest.

"Presidential letterheads are controlled items, sweetheart," he said, kissing the top of her head before he sat back down. "Jason Simcow, the chief of staff, immediately informed me of a mailing to Cali bearing the presidential seal. But, after reading the letter, I decided to allow it to go through. I had already interfered in Jessica's life enough," he said to Cara, apologetically. "I had to let the future rest in her hands."

They sat silently, watching the red sun descend in the direction of Cali, pink clouds floating on the horizon. "When did you know that she had decided her future?" asked Cara, putting her arm around Jessica's shoulder, rubbing her thumb against the silken flesh.

"Before you did, I think. It was in her voice. On the phone monitor. Her face told me. It began with your press briefing and escalated from there. By the time she visited me in Washington, DC, she was very much in love with you."

"Why didn't you tell her the truth at that time?" badgered Cara, not quite sure whether she should forgive this man.

"Because I didn't want to program her. She had to make her own decision by searching for the truth with you. That's what love is all about. It's a search for truth—something the first presidential occupant of this office never understood," he said angrily, his face screwed in contortions. "Patrick Olmstead was America's shame!" When he again spoke, his voice had returned to a normal level. "I know that you will be seeking Jessica's emigration to Cali. How do you propose to proceed?"

Cara outlined the plan Jody had prepared. "May we count on your help, Mr. President?"

"Definitely. I'll submit a statement to supplement Mrs. Anderson's. It never hurts to have the support of friends and family members in high places." His eyes twinkled. "Tell your friend Jody to coordinate her efforts with James Dowl. He's my personal attorney and can handle the legalities at this end."

Later, as they all sat at the dining room table while Mrs. Anderson, in a starched yellow apron, happily bustled about serving dinner, it was Tim who asked the question that had been concerning Cara. "After Jessica emigrates and the news hits the press, how will it affect your future as president?"

"Well," said President Mooran, peering over the glasses that sat on the tip of his nose, "I'm not sure how it'll affect my political future, but I know it'll make me a better president. It means I'll be able to do what I believe is right without fearing that the press will start digging into our family's past." He rested his arm lightly on the back of his daughter's chair. "I always worried about someone striking out at Jessica. Once it's out of the closet, I'll be able to stop worrying. Then, I can double my efforts to normalize relations with Cali. Hell, there are a lot of people out there, members of congress included, who've lost relatives to your country. Those people will understand why I tried to keep Jessica in the United States. They'll also understand the agonizing need of the American people to build normal alliances with the people of Cali. We need to take small steps in the right direction . . . out from under the shadows of Patrick Olmstead."

Cara, sitting on the other side of Jessica, nudged her in the ribs with her elbow. "Don't forget Sherry Ryan," she mumbled under her breath.

"Dad, there's a woman reporter we know who is as interested in improving relations with Cali as you. She even has an inside track to the prime minister. What do you think? Can you use her help?"

"Hell, yes! Just give her name and address to Simcow. I can use all the help I can get with Ekstrom. She's a tough old bear. You know,

Cara," he said, his voice softening, "I hope you'll be a little kinder to us when you're the prime minister."

Cara audibly gasped, almost choking on her own breath. "I don't know if that will ever happen, Mr. President, but if it does, it's a long way off. By then, you and Ms. Ekstrom will be old friends."

Mrs. Anderson, who had begun to clear the table, looked disapprovingly at the president, who had hardly eaten. He shrugged his shoulders. "That's always been my problem—I'd rather talk than eat. Well, I guess I'll be moseying off to my bedroom now. I still need to review the day's events, lest I give Simcow an excuse to scold me in the morning."

The three young people jumped to their feet as the president rose to say good night. "Cara," he said, removing his glasses as he hugged her to his chest, "I'll be leaving early in the morning, so I probably won't see you again before you depart for Cali. I want you to know how pleased I am that my daughter has chosen such a wonderful companion. It'll be my pleasure to take her to the *Fantasia* on the day of her emigration. And I look forward to the time when I can visit you both in your country."

"That will come, Mr. President."

"Well, my young friends," said Mrs. Anderson as the president disappeared from view, "It's past the time for me to rest my weary head, eh? So, I'll just be leaving these dishes where they are. I'll take care of it all in the morning." Removing her apron, she looked at Cara and winked.

"Will you love me forever?" asked Cara later in the privacy of the bedroom.

"Longer than that," responded Jessica, as she kissed her fervently. "And you? Will you always love me?" she asked as she held her around the waist.

Gently, Cara removed her hands and walked to the dressing table, returning with the small gift box. "Always," she said solemnly as they sat down on the divan in front of the blazing fireplace.

Sitting down, Jessica tugged off the gift wrap, her face softening as she slowed down to open the gray velvet box. Her breath caught as she looked at the bracelet. "It's beautiful."

"It's my heart," smiled Cara. The logs crackled warmly as she silently placed it on Jessica's wrist.

"Why the date January 1, 2056?" she asked as she turned the heart over, the silver flickering in the glow of the flames.

"I'm hoping you'll begin the new year with me in a commitment ceremony on January first." Cara picked up her braceleted hand. "I love your tiny fingers," she said as she kissed each one, eyes cast down, awaiting Jessica's response.

"That'll be a hard thing to do without my father there."

"Maybe by that time, he'll be allowed to be there." Pushing back the hair that fell carelessly across her forehead, she was beginning to doubt whether her proposal was going to be accepted.

"If he can't be there, can Barbra walk down the aisle with me?" Holding her hand out in front of her admiringly, she repositioned herself, resting her head on Cara's shoulder.

"As long as I'm at the other end, King Kong can walk down the aisle with you."

"Who is King Kong?" she giggled.

"That's a story for another day." Cara sighed. "Hey, where are you going?" she asked as Jessica suddenly jumped up and moved toward the door.

"I'm going to go pack our Ellyn Hargreaves records so she can sing to us during our ceremony."

"Forget it, my love," she said as she walked toward her and wrapped her up in her arms, her blonde hair reflecting goldenly in the glowing embers. "In Cali, the real thing will do the singing."

Thirty-Eight

On Saturday morning, Barbra telephoned. "I don't have good news, my dear."

Cara, hands numbing and muscles turning to mush, quickly flicked the switch to audible only and turned her back to Jessica who lay asleep at her side. "What do you mean?" she asked, feeling the chill of the damp September wind that gusted through the open window.

"Oh, my, don't be frightened my dear. It's not that terrible. No, not at all. It's just that I don't have an answer for you yet on Jessica's twin sister's Scarpetti records. I tried getting into the center several times this week. It was just too risky. There are too many people there on a normal workday who know me. So, it'll have to wait until tomorrow when only a skeleton staff will be on duty."

"What time Sunday?" asked Cara, stumbling over her words as Jessica began to show signs of awakening.

"It won't be until after your plane leaves. The center doesn't open till noon on weekends. I'm sorry, dear. I know how much this means to you. But don't you worry about a thing. I won't leave this country without an answer, and we'll get the answer to you somehow."

"I suppose there's nothing else we can do." Hearing the hammering of harsh rain, Cara pulled the phone across the bed to crank the window closed when she felt Jessica's gentle hands pulling her down on top of her. Too late, she covered her mouth to stifle a yelp.

"What's that? Did you say something else, dear?"

"No, it'll be okay," Cara answered, feeling her excitement mount with Jessica's strategically placed butterfly kisses.

"I'm sure it will. I'm sure everything will be just fine." Chuckling softly when she realized that she was listening to the activity of fore-

doi:10.1300/5559_39

play, Barbra barely managed to say good-bye before turning off her phone.

"You little devil," yelled Cara, looking down at Jessica who lay laughing with her eyebrow raised.

After a morning of lovemaking, Jessica lay on her back listening to the falling rain. "That's probably the next to last time we'll make love before I join you in Cali."

"Oh, did you have plans for tonight?" Leaning on her elbow, looking down at Jessica, Cara felt her heart surge. To know that she would be sharing her life with this woman filled her with a joy that extended through every fiber of her being.

"What do you think?" she asked with an impish grin, black ringlets tousled from the morning's activity.

Becoming serious, Cara gazed at the window, watching the droplets sway drunkenly in their tracks. "That was Barbra on the phone before. She won't be able to get into the Scarpetti Center today to verify that your sister's records are documented gene positive. She won't have an answer for us until after I leave on Sunday. I won't be here to celebrate with you."

"Do you have any doubts about the outcome?"

"No," lied Cara, not wanting to alarm Jessica into the realization that the legal proceedings would take longer and the commitment ceremony might have to be delayed if the twin's record did not support the statements of Mrs. Anderson and the president.

"Then let's celebrate right now while I show you why you shouldn't have any doubts," commanded Jessica as she pulled Cara back down on the bed.

Thirty-Nine

Sunday morning began bleakly. The raw rain pelted the windows as they arose to begin dressing in the September darkness.

"I wish there was a way to delay my departure time. I don't like leaving before Jocelyn's records are verified. My celebration should be here with you." Angrily, she pulled her Calian body suit from the hanger.

"It was! Or did you forget about yesterday?" asked Jessica with a familiar arch to her left eyebrow.

"Maybe I need a quick refresher course." Cara dropped her clothes and scampered across the bed, catching Jessica before she had a chance to move.

Twenty minutes later, they lay on the floor, still gasping for breath when Jessica stood up and put on her bathrobe. "I'd better go get my clothes or you really will miss that plane."

Cara stopped her at the door. "I don't think you should go with me to the airport."

Jessica looked at her quizzically, eyebrows furrowing over the dark gray eyes, saddened in disappointment.

"Come, sit next to me," said Cara, her heart breaking from Jessica's crestfallen countenance. She led her to the bed and sat down alongside, cupping her hand under Jessica's downcast chin. Tilting her head up, she lightly kissed the sensual cleft before she spoke. "Jessica, I come from a country where affection between two women is commonplace. For me to say good-bye to you at a public airport—not knowing how many weeks or months it may be before I see you again—and not be able to kiss you or embrace you with the passion that's in my heart would be more painful than I could bear. I'd rather

doi:10.1300/5559_40

leave you in this house—this wonderful house where the love grew. This is the memory I want us to nurture."

"How long do you think it will be before I am able to emigrate?" she asked, resting her head against Cara's breast.

"I don't know." She stroked her hair, her heart grimacing with pain.

"How will I be able to let you know when everything is okay? I'm not allowed to call. I can't write."

"You'll find a way," said Cara, kissing her forehead. "Now, you'd better leave before I forget my resolve."

"Just don't forget me." She jumped off the bed and was out the door before Cara was able to move.

"Never," she yelled through the open archway to the lithe figure running down the hallway.

Ignoring the emotions that were threatening to swallow her, she quickly dressed in Calian clothes and was ready when Tim came to the room. "It's time, beautiful. Will it just be the two of us?" he asked, looking around.

"Yes," she said simply.

When they reached the bottom of the stairs, they heard Mrs. Anderson bustling out of the dining room, yelling to them frantically. "Don't you be leaving without saying good-bye to me." Grabbing Tim by the collar, she almost lifted him off his feet as she pulled him in and, on her tiptoes, kissed him on both cheeks. "I'm sure going to be missing you, Mr. Felmar." Turning to Cara, she began to sniffle, tears running freely. "And you, Ms. Romero. You've become very special to me, eh? I know that Miss Jessica will be seeing you again. Do ya think I'll be so lucky?"

There are good-hearted people in America too, thought Cara, as she looked down at the caring tear-stained face. "I hope so, Mrs. Anderson. I certainly hope so."

Pulling Cara to her ponderous breasts, she squeezed tightly. "Please, please take care of my little leprechaun. She's been the light of my life. I can't imagine how dreary it will be here without her, but it will be better for me if I know she's happy. I will be giving you your statement, eh?"

"Thank you. And thank you for taking care of Jessica for the first twenty-nine years of her life. I promise I will take care of the rest." As she spoke, Mrs. Anderson's cheek against hers, she tasted the salt from their intermingling teardrops.

It was before 6:30 when they arrived at the airport, too early to draw attention from the crowds that had not yet gathered. Barbra and Sherry stood alone at the runway gate.

"I didn't expect you to be here," yelled Cara when she saw them. Throwing down her traveling bag and opening her arms wide, she ran toward Sherry, squeezing tightly as they hugged. "I thought I had missed you when I didn't see you at the conference center on Friday."

"No," said Sherry, smiling happily at the success of the surprise. "I wanted to be here to say good-bye privately, but I know this is not really good-bye. Jason Simcow already called me. And I'm going to see you again. If not next week, next month. If not next month, next year, but I will see you. And I will see my mother."

"Yes, you will."

"Cara, I don't know how to thank you. You've done so much for us. So much for me." In the background, Tim and Barbra were introducing themselves to each other.

"Just keep an eye on Jessica for me. Don't let her get discouraged by the burdens of the bureaucracy. That'll be thanks enough. Besides, I could never repay your mother for all that she's done on our behalf—"

"It seems to me, my dear, that it is I who owe you," interrupted Barbra. "You're every bit as wonderful as Miriam had described you when we were aboard the *Fantasia*. Miriam has always had excellent taste. Now, I will go to the Scarpetti Center this afternoon, and I've already informed Sherry that I will not leave here without Jessica." Cara looked at her with surprise. "You be sure to tell that to Miriam. If she wants me to share her bed with her, she had better use her influence with President Mooran. I'm not getting any younger, you know."

Embracing her tenderly, Cara laughed, whispering in her ear, "I am not sure I have the guts to say that to the prime minister in those exact words. I might have to modify them just a little."

"Why Cara, I do believe I've shocked you. I can feel your cheeks getting hot."

"I do believe you have," she said, squeezing tightly as she saw the pilot signal that the plane was ready to be boarded.

At 4:00 a.m., Cali time, they were on their way home.

Forty

—∽ঞ৯—

"I feel like a witch," said Cara as she watched Esther hang the Halloween decorations in the outer office.

"You're beginning to act like one." Standing on a step stool, she hung paper cutouts of pumpkins along the ceiling molding. "I have never seen you quite this cranky. You're biting off more heads than you can chew." Chuckling aloud, she climbed down. "I liked that line. I'm going to have to tell that one to Marge." Picking up two life-size cardboard witches that were almost hidden in her desk clutter, she hung one on each side of Cara's office door.

"You mean I'm going to have to look at that both coming and going?" Cara asked, sitting down in Esther's desk chair.

"Well, I could hang one on this side only—as a warning to people about to enter your office."

Cara leaned back in the chair, putting her feet on top of a crate of audio discs that sat alongside the desk. "You really should get rid of this crate. It makes the office look junky." Esther scowled at her, knitting her eyebrows together. "Damn, I have a right to be cranky. It's been three weeks since I left New York. I haven't heard from Jessica. Jody keeps telling me to be patient. President Mooran's attorney, whom I don't even know, is handling everything. Mother Sue is upset about the publicity that Jessica's arrival will generate. The PM is angry because Jessica's legal problems are holding up Barbra's emigration. I don't even know if the twin's record has been verified. And I'm worried." Sticking out her lower lip, she folded her arms across her chest with an exaggerated sigh and kicked the crate.

"I can't believe this is the mature Director of the Office for the Aging I see before me," commented Esther as she rummaged through the piles of paper on her desktop. "This came for you today," she said

 doi:10.1300/5559_41

as she grabbed a yellow sheet in the middle of a stack. "Tim Felmar's transfer came through. He'll be reporting in as your deputy director on November 15."

"Great! The way things are going, he'll probably get here before Jessica." Getting up, she marched back to her own office, glaring at the witch as she passed through the door. "I really am happy about Tim, though," she yelled over her shoulder.

Following behind, Esther pasted a sign, labeled "Ms. Romero" to the witch's chest. "I liked Tim very much, Cara, but don't you forget your promise to me. I will continue to be your escort officer for all your travels in Cali."

"Absolutely!" Cara said, flouncing down on her chair. "Tim accepted the assignment so he could stop traveling and spend more time with his future son. Just as soon as he's comfortable as deputy director, you and I will start making trips again. We've fallen way behind on inspections in the five months since the deputy's position has been vacant."

"Sounds good to me." Esther turned around and swiftly left the room, acting as though Cara would change her mind if she waited too long.

Alone in her office, smiling to herself with thoughts of Jessica, Cara jumped when Esther knocked on the open door.

"You really are preoccupied. Well, you'd better get your act together. The prime minister's office called. She wants to see you at two o'clock. That gives you," she looked at her watch, "eight minutes."

Grabbing her jacket, she put it on as she raced into the hall and bounded up the stairs. Damn, she thought as she ran, the PM must really be upset. She never calls on such short notice. She reflected back on their last conversation. Ekstrom had been very understanding of Cara's relationship with Jessica, demonstrating a rarely seen compassion. The only suggestion of anger occurred when Cara related that Barbra refused to leave the United States until Jessica was able to leave with her. "That woman will drive me crazy!" she yelled, glaring at the framed photograph that stood on the corner of her desk. "I've waited more than thirty-five years for her to come to this country, and she's going to keep me waiting some more."

"She's expecting you," said Jonathan, the receptionist, as Cara ran into the vestibule outside the prime minister's office. Jumping up from behind the desk, he pointed urgently to the open door.

The prime minister, who rarely displayed emotion, was pacing back and forth in the middle of the room, her head hanging down, oblivious to Cara's presence. Cara felt her knees stagger and her heart lurch drunkenly against her chest. There was something very wrong. "Ms. Ekstrom, you wanted to see me," she said loudly, running her fingers through her hair.

"Yes. Yes." She grabbed her by the hand and pulled her over to the transmission machine standing against the wall. "This terse message came through from President Mooran's office."

Cara grabbed the sheet of paper that the PM stuffed in her hand and hastily read it aloud. "Henry Mooran will hear the meadowlark sing on November first."

Collapsing into the chair that sat at the front of the prime minister's desk, Cara began to laugh, slowly at first, but more heartily with the passing moments. Doubling over, her hands pressed against the pain in her stomach, she lowered her head almost to her knees. Tears of laughter spattered the dark blue jacket.

"Cara," said the PM, trying to keep from chuckling, "I don't understand. What does this mean?" Laughing now, she tugged on Cara's sleeve. "You must tell me. What does this mean?" She sat down on the chair next to Cara and together, they laughed, slapping their hands against their knees, against one another, against the chair. Looking at the PM's contorted face, Cara laughed harder, setting Miriam into convulsive cackles. "Please, Cara, what does it mean?" she shrieked.

Gasping for breath, Cara finally spoke in labored phrases. "It means, Madame Prime Minister . . . that we . . . had better take you . . . to buy a pair of slippers."

ABOUT THE AUTHOR

Helen Ruth Schwartz was born and raised in New York City. She graduated from Queens College of the City University of New York with a bachelor of science degree. Shortly after her graduation, she accepted a commission as an officer in the Women's Army Corps, serving in the military for five years. Helen received the Army Commendation Medal for exceptionally meritorious service as the commanding officer of a Women's Army Corps unit, and later that same year, graduated from the Department of Defense Information School's journalism program as the Honor Graduate. When she returned to civilian life, Helen obtained her master of arts degree from the State University of New York at Stony Brook. As an avocation, Helen used her award-winning military skills to write for publications serving the gay and lesbian community. She supported her writing as a nursing home administrator, as a publisher of educational materials for nursing home administrators, and finally, as a real estate investor before retiring in order to devote her full time to writing. Helen currently lives in south Florida with Mollie, a yellow Labrador retriever. She is a member of the Federal Club of the Human Rights Campaign and is also a supporter of the Lambda Legal Defense and Education Fund.

HARRINGTON PARK PRESS®
Alice Street Editions™
Judith P. Stelboum
Editor in Chief

Past Perfect by Judith P. Stelboum

Inside Out by Juliet Carrera

Façades by Alex Marcoux

Weeding at Dawn: A Lesbian Country Life by Hawk Madrone

His Hands, His Tools, His Sex, His Dress: Lesbian Writers on Their Fathers edited by Catherine Reid and Holly K. Iglesias

Treat by Angie Vicars

Yin Fire by Alexandra Grilikhes

Egret by Helen Collins

Your Loving Arms by Gwendolyn Bikis

A Donor Insemination Guide: Written By and For Lesbian Women by Marie Mohler and Lacy Frazer

From Flitch to Ash: A Musing on Trees and Carving by Diane Derrick

To the Edge by Cameron Abbott

Back to Salem by Alex Marcoux

Extraordinary Couples, Ordinary Lives by Lynn Haley-Banez and Joanne Garrett

Cat Rising by Cynn Chadwick

Maryfield Academy by Carla Tomaso

Ginger's Fire by Maureen Brady

A Taste for Blood by Diana Lee

Zach at Risk by Pamela Shepherd

An Inexpressible State of Grace by Cameron Abbott

Minus One: A Twelve-Step Journey by Bridget Bufford

Girls with Hammers by Cynn Chadwick

Rosemary and Juliet by Judy MacLean

An Emergence of Green by Katherine V. Forrest

Descanso: A Soul Journey by Cynthia Tyler

Blood Sisters: A Novel of an Epic Friendship by Mary Jacobsen

Women of Mystery: An Anthology edited by Katherine V. Forrest

Glamour Girls: Femme/Femme Erotica by Rachel Kramer Bussel

The Meadowlark Sings by Helen R. Schwartz

Blown Away by Perry Wynn

Shadow Work by Cynthia Tyler

Dykes on Bikes: An Erotic Anthology edited by Sacchi Green and Rakelle Valencia

THE MEADOWLARK SINGS

_____in softbound at $16.95 (ISBN-13: 978-1-56023-575-0; ISBN-10: 1-56023-575-6)

Or order online and use special offer code HEC25 in the shopping cart.

COST OF BOOKS_____

☐ **BILL ME LATER:** (Bill-me option is good on US/Canada/Mexico orders only; not good to jobbers, wholesalers, or subscription agencies.)

☐ Check here if billing address is different from shipping address and attach purchase order and billing address information.

POSTAGE & HANDLING_____
(US: $4.00 for first book & $1.50
for each additional book)
(Outside US: $5.00 for first book
& $2.00 for each additional book)

Signature_____

SUBTOTAL_____

☐ **PAYMENT ENCLOSED: $**_____

IN CANADA: ADD 7% GST_____

☐ **PLEASE CHARGE TO MY CREDIT CARD.**

STATE TAX_____
(NJ, NY, OH, MN, CA, IL, IN, PA, & SD
residents, add appropriate local sales tax)

☐ Visa ☐ MasterCard ☐ AmEx ☐ Discover
☐ Diner's Club ☐ Eurocard ☐ JCB

Account # _____

FINAL TOTAL_____
(If paying in Canadian funds,
convert using the current
exchange rate, UNESCO
coupons welcome)

Exp. Date_____

Signature_____

Prices in US dollars and subject to change without notice.

NAME_____

INSTITUTION_____

ADDRESS_____

CITY_____

STATE/ZIP_____

COUNTRY_____ COUNTY (NY residents only)_____

TEL_____ FAX_____

E-MAIL_____

May we use your e-mail address for confirmations and other types of information? ☐ Yes ☐ No
We appreciate receiving your e-mail address and fax number. Haworth would like to e-mail or fax special discount offers to you, as a preferred customer. **We will never share, rent, or exchange your e-mail address or fax number.** We regard such actions as an invasion of your privacy.